Texas
Jack

BART HOPKINS

Printed by CreateSpace
North Charleston, South Carolina

Published by Bart Hopkins
Galveston, Texas

Library of Congress Control Number: 2013904985

ISBN: 1482373114
ISBN-13: 978-1482373110

DEDICATION

To Ryan, my buddy, the best son a father could have, times infinity.

ALSO BY BART HOPKINS

Fluke
Sweet Lenora (Paranormal Anthology with a Twist)

CONTENTS

Prologue: Early 1980s

Texas has more than its share of old farm roads. Some of them are used routinely and are well-traveled thoroughfares; some serve as shortcuts for people that live in the area; and believe it or not, some just connect one piece of farmland to another, providing a path for Mr. John Deere to go about his business on an early summer morning.

Other farm roads, however, escape notice. They no longer connect populated areas and they don't save anyone that ever-so-precious commodity of time. Entire days go by when no shadow falls upon the broken pavement. Four-legged creatures make unfettered excursions back and forth, here and there, without concern for the threats that plague so many other roadways, ending the tiny lives of critters prematurely. Those roads never completely cease to serve their purpose. They've just gotten old...like the farmer down the way. Time to get a glass of lemonade, go out to the porch, and sit for a spell. After all—everything deserves some peace now and then—even a road!

Sometimes, however, those roads are host to spectacles. Rowdy teenagers always seem to know about the unused spots and take advantage of them on the occasional weekend, leaving behind their telltale calling cards: an extra hole in the speed limit sign; tire tracks that disappear into the fields; or, a beer can in the knee-high grass along the road. Mostly it's harmless and expected: East Texas teenagers plus alcohol equals mild troublemaking.

If you were ever driving some of those East Texas farm roads in the 80s, you may have witnessed one of those spectacles. Like stumbling on a child's toy in the dark, it was probably under your feet before you knew what happened. If you were lucky, you didn't have time to figure it out, and you kept on your way.

If you weren't so lucky, you may have seen an old Dodge pick-up truck pulled over on the shoulder of the road. The truck was twenty years old by then, faded yellow, with simulated wood panels running its length. It may have even been sagging downward in the middle. Rust, neglect, and abuse had conspired to cripple the truck. It had seen better days.

Furthermore, you may have seen a young boy in the passenger seat of that downtrodden old truck, that rusty old beast. That boy would be urgently signaling to a man just off the side of the road when he noticed you approaching. Nothing escaped that boy's notice—he was eager to please his dad—and his mission was to let his dad know when a car was coming.

Now follow the twin, invisible rays from that boy's eyes to the object of all of his attention. They lead to a man in blue jeans and an un-tucked button-up. Mr. Blue Jeans would be standing *near* bushes if there were any, but plainly out in the open if that's how it had to be. Business is business, after all, and when you have to take care of business, there isn't room for pleasantries. Using bushes is merely being polite.

Anyone listening would have heard these words—the warning—shouted from the seat of the pick-up truck: "Dad, there's a car coming!"

A can of beer would be held nonchalantly in the man's left hand. In his mouth, a lit cigarette, bobbing softly up and down to the rhythm of some classic rock or country song as he sings softly to himself.

And, in his right hand? Why, it's his most prized possession, dangling out in the open for the world to behold, as he relieves himself very publicly without remorse or shame.

It's a crazy portrait—the finest of farm road spectacles indeed—a true phenomenon:

Hurry, hurry, hurry…step right up…catch a glimpse of the urinating, drinking, smoking, singing man with no shame! It's free to see and will stay with you forever!

If you weren't from around those parts, and you did not personally know my father, the threat of a heart attack might have had you swerving off the road once it really sank in, what you had witnessed. If you were from around those parts, you may have considered all of this normal. Wait…that isn't completely accurate. If you were from around those parts, *and you knew this man*, then you might think it was normal.

That man was Bill Leonard. William if you were his mom or his wife. Billy if you were anyone else. That boy hollering a warning through the window was Jack, Billy's son. He was only trying to penetrate the hundred-proof haze—puncture that invisible membrane of awareness—and alert his inebriated father.

I'm that boy: Jack Leonard. I apologize if I didn't warn him in time and you had to see all of that. Sometimes I was successful and other times I was not. Even when I got his attention in time, there was no way to determine whether he would speed up, stop, or seek cover. That was his way and that was how things were.

Now, don't let that give you the wrong impression of Texas. That behavior isn't Texas; that behavior is Billy Leonard.

I grew up in Texas and it's not always what people imagine. It is sometimes, but not all the time. I don't wear a Stetson, my belt buckle was average in size, and I preferred almost any shoes to boots. My life was absent the stereotypical horses, manure, and barn. I could *see* the horses, manure, and barn, but only in the distance when we drove by. I even managed to avoid acquiring an accent.

I do have one Texas confession: I love guns and football. Not at the same time—separately—but, we'll talk more about those things later.

We moved from the small town where I was born when I was eight years old and I spent the rest of my formative years in the city of Houston. Key word: city. There were still those that chose to make Red Wings and Wranglers part of their wardrobe, but for the most part, in the *city* of Houston, they were either poseurs or they just liked that style of clothing. There were real cowboys, sure, but they didn't grow up with me or live on my block.

I remember my first day of school. As much as an eight-year-old boy can feel the differences in culture created when moving to a new place, I felt it. The world was concrete and glass and I felt like one of the Beverly Hillbillies. I remember watching reruns of that show when I was young, but in Houston I felt like I might be starring in my own episodes.

"Redneck" was one of several nicknames given to me by peers. I didn't mind it (much); I had a saving grace. I was a natural when it came to sports. Any sport, I could pick it up quickly. For fear of underestimating more than half of the planet, I would wager that most women never understand the unifying power of sports for men and boys. Some men don't understand it either, and I couldn't have verbalized it at the time, although I was familiar with what was transpiring. I knew that something was different and I knew it was a product of the proverbial jock strap. My shortcomings disappeared on the fields.

"Redneck" evaporated my first year in Houston and I became just one of the guys. A few closer friends still messed with me, but with a fondness not present before.

My house was large, and we had a pool, which added to my status among my classmates. Billy Leonard had inherited a tidy sum of money when his own father, Seth, passed away. Grandpa Seth had been killed in an accident at the Texas City plant he worked at most of his life and I had only a vague memory of him. It was a freak accident—one that shouldn't have happened. As such, the insurance payout was large.

But, as the saying goes, "You can take the boy out of the country, but you can't take the country out of the boy." For my father, that held true after our change in fortunes. He dressed better, his house was better, and I suppose in some ways, he improved in other areas of his life. But, he was still the same guy underneath. He continued to drive with a beer in his hand, feeling that as a *man*, it was not only his right, but that it was somehow…okay. Steering the vehicle seemed more of an afterthought after his music, beer, and cigarettes.

Something he did abstain from was roadside urination. He no longer pulled over to *drop trousers* and *water grass*. He was an upstanding citizen now and couldn't visibly undermine the sanctity of a densely populated area in society, could he? Well, let's not go overboard and give Billy that much credit. Houston is the land of a million bathrooms. It's probably harder to stop on the side of the highway; you'd likely be fined for it. Gas stations, malls, and restaurants were everywhere and had restrooms. Availability and the threat of jail time were effective deterrents for my dad, no doubt.

When we moved out of the *country,* I realized for the first time that my dad's behavior was not only illegal, but morally questionable. Drinking and driving weren't a good match; however, he was my dad so I figured he knew something I didn't.

My father had trained me well as a tike. Warn him if cars are coming, but make *damned* sure I get his attention if *police* cars are coming. I thrived on positive attention from my father. To get this attention, I had to take part in his world. I learned how to open a can of beer and bring it to him at the age of two. I learned how to identify police cars, so that I could warn my dad of their approach, as he produced 16 ounces of liquid on the side of the road. My dad was a man on terms with no one else. To be a significant part of his life meant climbing the fence and joining him on his side. And that's what I did.

Chapter 1
Tuesday Morning, July 31ˢᵗ, 2012

I walked over to my office window and watched the sun rise behind downtown Austin. It appeared bigger today than most days, as if it had moved closer to Earth. *Or perhaps Earth had moved closer to it,* I mused. It was a brilliant yellow—a ball of lemony golden fire—something I had not seen very often.

The view from my window wasn't the best in the building, but it was good; it was very good. They say it's good to be the king. Let me tell you: it's also good to be the king's assistant. I was in charge of marketing and public affairs for the company, which had a variety of perks, and a really great view of the city was one of them.

I watched the sun for a little while. Calm mornings were pretty critical to me. Some people needed caffeine; I needed Zen time. I cast my eyes down, away from the bright blues and yellows of the celestial dome. Along the street in front of my building, grays and greens were the pervasive hues this morning. They weren't unpleasant colors. They were calming; they were welcoming. Sidewalks, street signs, and patches of grass lined the building. People were starting to walk up and down the street, each seeking their own relevancy in their own way. I began to see small bursts of color here and there: sunglasses; purses; ladies' shoes. The occasional suit. Lots of polo-styled shirts. A brilliant red dress that was really too striking for morning time and would be better suited for a night on the town in Gotham with Bruce Wayne.

I picked up my bottle of water, twisted off the lid, and took a long drink. I felt completely at ease. Pretty soon the work for the day would start. Unless acted upon by an outside force, my days were good when I started off in a relaxed frame of mind. It was the reason I always came to work early.

My phone vibrated a few times from its normal spot on

the desk behind me, indicating a new text. I looked down to the street once more and noticed a very large man wearing a very small shirt. *Little brother's shirt,* I chuckled to myself. All the clothes available in this world and that guy picked a shirt three or four sizes too small. *I wonder if that really impresses anyone,* I thought and chuckled again. I pulled the curtains closed on my Zen time, and strolled over to my desk. It was time to start working anyway.

My wife's picture greeted me from my phone. It was a great shot, taken at the base of the Eiffel Tower on our honeymoon. Samantha was laughing and pushing a hand through her hair. It was the best kind of photograph—unplanned and unposed—a truly candid and beautiful moment snatched from time. It was also my favorite picture of her—what I considered the perfect representation of my wife's life: energetic and happy.

I read Samantha's message:

I'll be home late, I really have to get this medical software done if we are going to Houston next week. Are we still going? Also - Can you pick up Jacob from Ryan's house? Love you!

We had been talking about this trip to Houston to see my parents. My sister Katie, her husband Mike, and their kids were going to be there for a few days, so it seemed like perfect timing. We were all overdue for some relaxation and we owed Jake another trip to see his grandparents before school started. Plus...I was anxious to see the new Historic Pleasure Pier in Galveston, or "G-town" as my friends and I had called it back in high school. I had seen pictures on the Galveston Facebook page and thought that it might be a fun place to take Sam for a date night.

It was a pretty normal trip; nothing out of the ordinary. But, it was hard to clear our schedule more than a few times each year. My parents traveled our way, too, but only so often due to my mother's volunteer activities. She lived to give.

Since it was already Tuesday, I jotted a note to myself to firm up our plans. My parents had plenty of room and I had already requested the vacation days. It seemed like a no-brainer.

Definitely going to Houston, I punched into the phone, *and I will grab Jake on my way home. Don't forget to add that coding we talked about. Love u too.*

Even though it bothered me on some level to use shortened words in texts, I had to admit that it made things a little quicker…a little easier…even though I guess it only amounted to a few wasted seconds to spell out words. I only hoped humanity didn't altogether forget how to spell in the future, after technology had burrowed into our lives for a while.

My wife worked for a software company that created *custom business solutions* for clients. That translated into writing tailored software applications for those clients. Samantha was the Michelangelo of software creation at her company, consistently sought out by name. She was a technical expert, creative and friendly, and could intuit what people wanted with minimal input.

Her current project was a medical database. She had described it to me a few weeks ago when we were having lunch.

"It's going to be really good," she had said. "It's going to completely marry patients, their medical history, and their billing. Different users will be able to log in, and according to their account permissions, they'll be able to see what is pertinent, or appropriate, for their position in the practice's hierarchy."

"To help protect privacy act information and that sort of thing?" I had asked.

"It's going to safeguard everything. No one will see anything that they shouldn't. We're also talking about extending this to patients…giving them access to their records from the Internet. Of course, that gets a little trickier. The Internet isn't a closed medium."

"I think I have an idea that could really be fantastic," I said.

"Oh, yeah?" she asked, her tone becoming *almost* playful, but not quite. She was testing the water to see what temperature it was. She knew me very well and suspected a joke in the making. But, she could never be sure.

"Yes. I was thinking you could introduce some code that randomly inserts sexually transmitted diseases into patient profiles."

"You think that would be funny?"

"I do. I think it would be very funny. Maybe add a notation that the spouse needs to be notified right away so that they can be tested as soon as possible."

"Okay," Samantha had said, nodding her head. "I'll add it today."

"You will NOT be sorry," I said and nodded back at her.

Text sent, I sat down at my desk and turned on my computer. Email dominated the first hour or so of each of my workdays. Most of the guys I worked with complained about all of the emails they received. On the one hand, I could understand their complaints:

We never just talk to each other anymore…

I'm always getting spammed with email about office fundraisers…

Just pick up the phone and call me!

On the other hand, I didn't feel the same way about email as they did. I mean, sure, now and then it seemed like a burden; I received twice as many as was truly needed. Maybe more. And it was another thing for the must-be-done list each day.

Most of the time, however, I thought email was a wonderful system for recordkeeping. It also served as proof, or evidence, of everything we did. Not to mention it was exceptionally handy for coordinating and planning.

Perhaps, and most importantly…I found that it helped

guys whose memory seemed to be routinely inadequate (me). I relied on sticky notes, lists, and calendars to make it through the day. My Outlook calendar was my Yoda, providing guidance and reminders: the mental *whack!* I frequently needed.

So I never (mostly never) opened email with a heavy heart and today was no exception. The only shocking thing about opening Microsoft Outlook today was the lack of anything substantial. A few memorandums were floating around for informational purposes. Otherwise, not much at all. The day was off to a good start indeed. I leaned back in my chair and looked at the framed photo on my desk.

My wife and son smiled at me. They were standing next to a swimming pool. Samantha had her right arm around Jake's shoulders and her left arm lifted up triumphantly, hand thrown up showing a big number one. Jake was in his trunks, grinning bashfully, with his right hand lifted up, a mirror image of his mom's: #1!

I grinned back at them in the picture. It was taken during this last school year. Jake had joined a local, after-school swim team and he had demonstrated natural talent. He was better than the other 10-year-olds and could give many of the bigger kids a run for their money. They had several competitions through the year and he won in his age group at each. I was excited about the coming year since there was a 6th grade team. It reminded me of my own high school football days. Like father, like son.

I picked up my iPhone and swiveled around to my little stereo. Samantha surprised me with it last year, when I really got into all of the iStuff that seemed to be taking over our galaxy. The stereo had a dock for charging and playing the full gamut of iGadgetry from iPods to iPads. I slapped the iPhone into it and hit *shuffle*.

A moment later Nirvana came out of the speakers and I found myself entering the not-so-distant realm of nostalgia. I looked again at Samantha and Jacob. I probably wasn't going to accomplish much today in this weird, retrospective mood. Best just to let it all take me away.

Chapter 2
1993

My freshman year at Texas A&M nearly killed me. It was the first time that I had been away from my parents for more than a handful of days. It was less than a three-hour drive, but it felt like an entire universe had been bridged.

I was offered a few minor sports scholarships, but opted not to participate in athletics that year, to the disappointment of several high school coaches. Instead, I focused on two of the more traditional Leonard family activities—drinking and heavy drinking. The apple doesn't fall far from the tree, right? A typical day went something like this:

1) Wake up to a chorus of electronic beeps and the local radio station.
2) Stay awake with pharmaceutical assistance as required (ephedrine).
3) Set three alarm clocks again for the next morning.
4) Scramble to finish homework, often by acquiring the answers from more studious friends and roommate.
5) Attend classes and try to remain coherent.
6) Come back to apartment.
7) Start getting hammered.
8) If possible, find girl, get drunk, and see where things end up. If girl discovery was not possible, proceed with the getting hammered part again.
9) Pass out.
10) Repeat steps 1-9.

Steps two through six of my *routine* were deleted on the weekends. The scary thing was the number of guys I knew that were living like this, too, with only slight variations in their own *routines*. You'd think that we were recently released from prison instead of being freshly arrived from middle class homes.

Scott Thompson was my roommate. We had been friends since I moved to Houston. A tall guy, 6'4", with a thick shock of red hair, he was built like a brick wall and sort of looked like one. We had played football together for the last decade. Well, until this year, anyway.

"Jack! Your mom's on the phone! Wake up!" Scott hollered through my door. I only halfway heard him, still drunk from the night before, and I didn't think that I could muster the energy to move. I decided that I was just dreaming and fell back asleep. I didn't hear the door as it creaked open seconds later, but I couldn't miss the 235 lbs. that slammed into my world.

"Shit, bro..." I croaked, rolling, trying to get the big bastard off of me.

"Dude. Your room stinks like old beer and warm ass," he observed. If my head weren't being pummeled on all sides by shockwaves of hang-over pain, I might have laughed. "Get up, man. Mommy's on the phone." He elbowed me a couple of times in the back, sat on me a little bit longer, then stood up and promptly ripped the blanket off of me. The cold air hit my body in an ugly way and I was forced to get up quickly. The odd thing is that my headache disappeared right after that. Small blessings, small blessings.

I grabbed my green robe off the floor, threw it on so that hypothermia wouldn't kick in, and made my way to the phone in the living room. "Hey, Mom," I said when I picked it up. Scott lounged in the chair by the television, protein shake in one hand, remote control in the other, and flipped to a local news channel.

"Jacky. Are you doing okay? You sound bad," she said, matter-of-factly.

"I'm fine, Mom. I was still asleep."

"Honey, it's almost two in the afternoon!" she replied. My eyes scanned the wall and found our clock: 1:50 pm. Wow—I was becoming a zombie.

"Yeah...I wasn't feeling too good..." I lied quickly, not really knowing why I had lied at all. She wasn't oblivious to the famous Leonard pastimes, which led to sleeping late.

"Well," she said, pausing only slightly, "I hope you feel better soon."

"Yeah. I'm sure I will. Just burning the midnight oil this week...had a few exams." Another inexplicable lie. I had the intense desire to keep most of my life hidden from my parents. I couldn't explain it—it was not a conscious decision—but something I felt compelled to do nonetheless.

"Well, I am sure you did well," she said, thankfully not mentioning the decline my grades had taken in the high school-to-college transition.

"So, what's going on, Mom?"

"Oh, the same old things, I guess. Your dad and his buddies think that Bill Clinton and the Brady Bill are going to lead to the total loss of freedom in America. Don't get me wrong, you know that *I* am a Republican, too, just like your father, but he and his little friends can really forget their manners." She usually had some nugget of information to toss out about my dad and his political views. It was one of the few things that could distract him from his malted grain and hops for more than a few minutes and sour his normally happy-go-lucky demeanor.

"And work is great—you know how I love the kids. Kaitlyn is doing really well," she added. My baby sister was in high school. Katie—in the same way that I was a natural at sports—was natural at just being wonderful. She was the happiest person that I knew, with a temperament that never visibly ruffled.

"We always knew Katie would be dynamite."

"She is a pleasant kiddo," Mom agreed. "What day will you be here for Christmas break?"

"We get out on the 17th...so I should be there a day or two after that. I think. Scott and I are probably going to ride in his car and he'll just drop me off." Feeling a little more awake, I snagged a pen from the counter and threw it at Scott. In a characteristically accurate throw, it bounced off the side of Scott's head. Unshaken, he raised the hand nearest me and extended his middle finger, but kept his eyes on the television.

"That sounds good, dear. You know we love Scott." In the history of mankind, there was no truer statement. My mother loved that he was polite and well mannered. My dad liked most of my friends, but he was especially fond of Scott for three reasons.

First, Scott was a great football player. His long strides made him fast and his size made him formidable. He was fierce. I owed him for my own success on the field.

Second, Scott loved to *shoot*. He enjoyed spending a Saturday afternoon at one of the ranges putting rounds through his rifle or pistols. And, he was really good at it: safe and accurate. This was, indeed, exactly like my dad. Well, not exactly. Scott didn't sneak beer into the range or bring a cooler out to the deer blind.

Third, Scott was passionate about cleaning his firearms. This particularly impressed my dad, who had inherited the same habit from his own father. They would solemnly and meticulously, almost lovingly, break down and clean them. While I was functionally competent, their enthusiasm (love) for the cleaning process baffled me.

"Well, I love you, Mom."

"I love you, too, dear. And your dad loves you. He'll probably call you sometime this week. He mentioned that he wanted to talk to you about something."

"Okay, Mom. Love you. Bye."

"Bye, Jacky." I hung up the phone, because one of the odd quirks about my mom was that she would *never* hang up the phone first. You could hear the line stay open on the other end. It felt like a staring contest...except there was no contest at all because she never backed down.

I put the phone down and for the first time since I started college, I thought that it might be nice to go home for a few days.

"How's Lainey?" Scott asked, giving me a wink, and lifting his eyebrows twice in quick succession. "She missing what I used to give her?"

"You mean that little wiener you have?"

"No, dude. I mean the gigantic sausage in my pants." He smirked again and knocked back the rest of his shake. I shook my head and we both laughed.

That's when I remembered we had a concert to go to that night. "Dude, we're gonna be watching Nirvana in a few hours. It's pretty much gonna be amazing!"

"It *is* going to be amazing." Scott agreed. He stood up, walked to the kitchen, and rinsed out his glass. "I can't believe we were able to get tickets. I thought for sure it would be sold out. Do you want to drive?"

"Sure. We have to leave soon, man. You know how stupid parking is. Maybe we can go bummin' on the way."

Bumming was the practice of scouting convenience stores for *those in need* and offering them cash in exchange for buying booze. It was less risky and usually more successful than trying to buy beer with fake and borrowed IDs.

And, while Scott was a convincing 21 at 19, I wasn't. I was cursed with the face of a baby, and while not unpleasant, I didn't exactly exude rugged, mature vibes or whatever magic was needed to buy alcohol. No measure of bullshit, and no amount of identification modification changed the fact that I had the face of a 16-year-old.

"That sounds appropriate, brother. Let's gear up!"

~~~~~

We were on the outskirts of Hempstead, moving slowly, looking for the right convenience-store-and-bum combination.

"Okay. Let's try this one," Scott said, pointing at the 7-Eleven coming up on our right. There was a man tucked almost out of sight along the wall on the side of the small building. I lifted the turn-signal bar in my Bronco II, easing onto the street adjacent to the store. The green arrow on the dashboard clicked a few times and shut off. *Right turn, right turn, right turn, good.* "Target acquired," Scott added.

The guy propping up the wall certainly *looked* destitute. His clothes were threadbare with visible holes. He hadn't moved since we first laid eyes on him and I wondered briefly if he was asleep (or dead). I slowed to a speed so low that the speedometer didn't register it, while Scott rolled down his window. We stopped alongside the curb, maybe 15 feet from the guy.

"Hey, buddy," Scott called out. It seemed like a ridiculous thing to say. It *was* a ridiculous thing to say. That man wasn't Scott's buddy. But, it sounded natural coming from Scott. He had a way about him that got to people, attracted them. *Who calls a bum 'buddy?'* I wondered.

The man moved for the first time, slowly raising his right hand, sipping from a bottle he held there. He either wasn't aware that Scott had spoken, or he was ignoring us. I was betting 50-50 either way.

"Hey, buddy...can you help us out?" Scott persisted. His voice bridged the narrow gap between my vehicle and the man. I watched a spark of recognition flash in the man's eyes so visibly it was cartoonish. He smiled broadly, revealing multiple gaps where teeth were once located (ages ago, no doubt), and hobbled over to the passenger side of my car.

"Whaddaya say there, young fellas?" the old guy

rasped, leaning into the open window.

A ghastly smell immediately invaded my Bronco. While invisible, the brute force and palpability of the odor was surprising. My initial reaction was to flee, to hide, to go anywhere that wasn't right here next to some damned 7-Eleven, where a homeless man parked himself. I was a fan of Stephen King and this was the kind of odor that he might write about. It always preceded the unveiling of evil in his books and it usually resulted in death. My stomach did a small somersault then righted itself.

"Hey, buddy...do you think you can pick up a 12-pack for me and my friend here?" Scott asked him. He held up a $10 bill. "Keep the change?" Scott didn't appear phased in the slightest by the stench. On the contrary, while bile loaded the back of my throat, threatening release, Scott was smiling at the guy.

"Ohhh! I see, I see." He stepped away from the window, tilted the amber bottle in his hands, and drained the remaining liquid. "Looks like I *need* a new drink. Whatchoo want?"

"Cheap beer, buddy," Scott told him, handing over the money. *There it is: buddy #4!* I thought. The man took the bill and shuffled off around the corner of the store. I kept the truck idling but put my window down to get some new air circulating inside.

"Think we're good?" I asked, drumming my fingers impatiently on the steering wheel. It's funny...I never felt uneasy *drinking* the beer, but I always felt uneasy *buying* the beer. I was always paranoid that we would be busted, cops waiting around every corner to haul us *downtown*. And even if the cops didn't show up, who could account for the craziness of the homeless? For all I knew, we were going to be the victims of a savage attack.

"I got a good feeling."

"What about that god-awful stink? Your boy could use some soap."

"Yeah. There's no denying he could use a shower," Scott replied. He leaned forward and tapped his fingers on the dashboard and started humming. It sounded like *All Apologies* from Nirvana's *In Utero* album. *Always a good choice,* I thought.

Just then, our guy came cruising back around the building holding a 12-pack in one hand and the standard brown-bag-and-bottle combo in the other. It may have been my imagination, but it looked like he had a new spring in his step. Scott smiled affably as 144 ounces of Natural Light got passed through the window.

The smell of the living dead danced around the vehicle again, but not as strong, thanks to my open window. I grimaced but gave a "hey, thanks" smile as best I could.

Scott cracked open his first beer while I pulled back out onto the main road. "Natty Light?" he asked.

"Nah. I'll wait until we get parked." After all, this wasn't 1980 and I wasn't my dad, though the resemblance was uncanny otherwise. My friends thought more like my father in these regards.

"Well, here's to you then, my designated driver for our journey to Nirvana. Hey, where's the cassette cover, ha-ha!" He laughed and slapped his leg.

I immediately knew what he was talking about. I withdrew the cassette box from the storage bin, in the center console, and tossed it across the seat. It was from the *Nevermind* album, which had been a favorite of ours in high school. We blared it before every game that one year. But, the cover of the album was a little ridiculous.

"Ha, ha! You can see his little pecker, man. Just right there in the water!" Scott laughed again loudly and I joined him. I mean, it *was* funny. Scott's guffaws were a little over the top, but once he got going, it was hard to stop him.

Scott laughed more as he popped out the cassette and put it in the tape deck. He took a long pull from his can and settled back. What was coming next wasn't optional. There were two primary rules that must be followed on concert nights.

One, it was mandatory before any concert that you listen to music from that band en route to the show. If this was not possible (and there weren't many acceptable excuses) then some time during that day was fine. This was really about setting the mood and getting psyched up.

Two, it was highly encouraged that you wear a band t-shirt to all concerts. It could be from any band – that part didn't matter. Scott's shirt tonight was from U2, more than acceptable at any show, while Helmet was emblazoned across my own chest.

We didn't create the rules, though we had mulled over them, and decided that we agreed with them.

Those guidelines having been followed, we were well on our way to a successful night. I glanced over at Scott as music filled my Ford.

Scott opened up another beer and tilted it back, smacking loudly, intentionally. "It's like canned heaven, the Natty Light. God bless it, God bless it. Only the best for two Texas boys out for the night."

Only the best…right! I thought, shifting gears, picking up speed.

The drive was uneventful and soon enough we were there. I parked the car in one of the various parking lots that surrounded the arena. We had been blaring music and driving for the better part of an hour and the silence when I cut the engine was a little startling. "Say, you don't have to be a Rockefeller to help a feller…pass me a beer," I said.

Scott passed me a Natural Light and we sat quietly for a few moments, watching rivulets of teenagers and twenty-somethings make their way across the parking lot to join the river of people along the main road. There were a few outliers, but for the most part, people seemed to follow the same paths to get to the road. It seemed symbolic of nature in general.

"Lots of hotties," Scott said. I agreed.

"Also a lot of dudes."

"Always a lot of dudes," he said. He finished what I was guessing was his fifth beer. We had been drunk together many times and I knew he was still good. My father didn't know Scott could hold his liquor the way he did, but even if he did know, it would just be another notch in Scott's favor. My dad respected a man that could hold his liquor.

We knocked back another couple of beers each and listened to several tracks on Nirvana's *In Utero*. It had only been a couple of months since I bought it, but I was really starting to dig it. I especially liked *All Apologies*.

In the sun I feel as one...

"Let's join the herd!"

~~~~~

The music was loud. Scott and I peeled off our shirts and quickly made our way up front. We were in the pit during most of the opening band's sets. Jostling, bumping, pushing...same scenario we'd been through a dozen times together at other shows. We watched out for each other, keeping an eye open for the random nitwit that would get overzealous and swing an elbow with the intent to hurt someone.

Tonight was going well—only minor bruising and no troublemakers. I decided the music, while okay, wasn't memorable; I thought it unlikely that the band would progress beyond being an opening act even though opening for Nirvana was impressive.

I motioned to Scott and he leaned in close. "Hey, man, I'm going to go get some water!" I shouted. "The place we saw in the back over there..." I pointed in the general direction from which we had entered the main area. He nodded and I started pushing my way through the pit crowd. The smell of bodies was strong, and not completely disagreeable, though sometimes you did smell putrid body odor. Underneath the human smells, I caught a whiff of marijuana. This wasn't any big surprise to me. In my high school, pot had been easier to get your hands on than alcohol. It never really appealed to me though. I stood by my old pal: beer. We had known each other a long time. Now and then, I went for the stronger stuff— whiskey or bourbon—but it never satisfied me like beer.

I broke free from the densely packed mass of people closest to the stage and found myself out in the regular crowd. Generally, people were more peaceful, less preoccupied with jumping, crowd-surfing, and all that other stuff the farther away from the stage that you got. I enjoyed it up close in the frantic craziness, in small doses, but always needed a few breaks. Otherwise I would have gone crazy. And, then, maybe that's what was wrong with everyone else.

The makeshift bars and plywood sales stands beckoned me. I obliged the calling and found myself checking out the *In Utero* tour shirts. I figured that I should probably wait and buy one at the end of the night so that I wouldn't have to hold onto it. The rub was that I would have to wait in line if I bought it later instead of now. As I picked at stuff here and there, I noticed a girl at the other end of the booth.

There had not been many moments in my life when the world stopped moving around me—moments when everything in the periphery blurred or disappeared. There had been a few, but mostly only what I would call my high school football moments.

But, this...this was different.

I'm not even really sure if I was breathing. She was gorgeous. I watched her look through different shirts, light brown hair to her shoulders. Shoulders, which of course, were tanned a soft golden brown and unblemished. I tried to get control of myself. My involuntary bodily functions faltered. I forced myself to pull in oxygen. *Breathe in. Breathe out. Breathe in. Breathe out.* People were bumping into me periodically. Some guy nearby was giving me a dirty look—no idea why. Maybe I was in his way. I nodded my head in an ambiguous way, which could mean, "excuse me" or "hey," as I edged closer to *her* end of the table. He gave an equally ambiguous nod of his own. I interpreted it as an acceptance of my quasi-apology. I don't know for sure, because after that, I couldn't take my eyes off of the girl.

She looked in my direction and an electric charge passed through me. She smiled at me. I kept it together and smiled back. It felt like a stampede of wild beasts were running in my chest, but it was only my heart. She looked back at the shirts tacked in squares along the booth. I couldn't be sure, but it looked as if her cheeks had colored and gotten darker. I looked back at the shirts, too. I saw colors, I saw patterns, I saw letters.

But, I never really focused on anything. I had no idea what was on the shirt in front of me. I was looking at it, but I wasn't looking at it.

I lifted my head slowly and looked her way again. My mind was swimming. Everything seemed to be simultaneously in perfect focus and yet hard to see. She looked up again, and I walked over to her. And...stood dumbly before her for several seconds.

Thankfully, she broke the extended silence, "Hi. I'm Samantha," she said.

"Jack. I'm Jack," I replied, nodding, trying to recover my senses. I didn't remember walking over to her. I couldn't take my eyes off of her face. She was breathtaking. The softest, yet most intense, brown eyes looked back at me. Full lips that weren't too dry or wet, big or small, just perfect. Her tanned skin radiated a healthy glow with a subdued sensuality that made my heart beat faster. I regained some of my composure, and always the joker, asked, "Come here often?"

Luckily, she heard what I said for what it was: bad humor. "Actually, it's my first time here. Do *you* come here often?"

"If you were here, I would." I winced inwardly. It was possibly the first unplanned, non-contrived come-on that I had used on a girl. An honest answer that probably sounded like a bad line. She blushed then, and I realized she knew the truth. I found that I had even shocked myself with the answer.

"Would you?" she asked.

"I would." I said, without hesitation or doubt.

"That's really nice...Jack." She said my name like it was a car she were taking for a test drive. She was so beautiful it was hard to look away. So, I didn't.

"Are you from Houston?" I asked.

"No. I'm going to school here. What about you?" she said.

"Sort of...we moved here when I was young." I replied. "Where *are* you from?"

"It's so small, you've never heard of it."

"Try me. Is it in Texas?"

"Yes. It's a little town called Iraan."

"Iran?"

"No...IRA...AN...like the names Ira and Anne, put together."

"Ira-an."

"Yep."

"You're right, I've never heard of it," I said, laughing.

"Nobody has heard of it." She laughed, too. Her eyes, even in the dim room were sparkling. "Are you here with anyone?"

"Yeah, I'm here with my buddy, Scott. He's out there somewhere," I told her, waving my hand in the general direction of the crowd. "Are you here with anyone?"

"My friends, Raquel and Jackie," she said, nodding her head only the slightest bit with the music.

We were both raising our voices to be heard, but it wasn't too bad. Of course, I'm not sure anything really mattered to me at that moment. The only thing that I was focusing on was Samantha.

"Do you have something against shirts?" she asked. I saw her eyes move to my chest and linger briefly before moving back up, and I realized that I still had my shirt tied around my waist. The look in her eyes was playful. She was messing with me, which I took as a good sign. Still, I was instantly self-conscious about being shirtless even though I was in good shape and normally would try to find an opportunity to take my shirt *off*. A pretty girl has the power to do that—shake the firmest ground like an earthquake—make you do the things that you normally wouldn't do and spin your world around.

"Ha ha...that's right, that's right. Shirts are for girls." As I said that, I groaned inwardly at how lame I probably sounded. I took my Helmet shirt from around my waist and pulled it over my head.

She smiled though, which made me feel better. I was

actually still shell-shocked about the situation. She was, without a doubt, the most beautiful girl I had ever seen. And here we were. I didn't go to Nirvana concerts to meet women; nobody did, as far as I knew. This was just supposed to be another drunk night hanging out with Scott.

Yet, here I was.

"Do you want to get a drink?" I asked her, pointing at the booth nearby. "Water, I mean? Water?"

"Yes. Water is actually what I am *supposed* to be getting for Raquel and Jackie. And me. I just got sidetracked by the shirts, and…"

"And by a really good looking guy?"

"Maybe." She looked at me and our eyes met and locked. It made my stomach tighten up and tingle. In the old movies, you'd hear Tarzan right about now.

We made our way to the drink booth and I ordered five waters. We chatted some more and everything was good. I eventually stopped trying to make things go right, and the natural rhythm of two people connecting took over.

"Can we meet up, after the show?" I asked her, finishing my bottle of water.

She looked at me over the rim of her water and crinkled her eyes. I thought she was interested, but she was hesitating. "Yeah. That would be good."

"Okay. What about right here or at the t-shirts?"

"The t-shirts make sense…" she said. "After all, shirts are for girls."

Well, I guess remembering a bad joke was better than *not* being remembered at all. "Cool. I'll see you then."

We parted ways toward different sides of the arena. I looked back once, to see if she was still visible. She was. Not only that…she looked back at the same time.

~~~~~

I found Scott and gave him the extra water that I had bought when I was talking to Samantha. He chugged it down rapidly. I'm not even sure he stopped to breathe. I noticed that a relatively disgusting volume of sweat was pouring off of him. He was like that sometimes when we were playing football and he routinely lost 5-10 lbs. during a tough game. I always gave him grief for being such a sweaty bastard.

"What's up, bro? You look like Bambi or something."

"What? Bambi?"

"Yeah, man. Look at you. What just happened? Did you meet a guy or something? You look all flushed and excited like maybe you met a guy."

"Ha ha ha, punk." I said lamely. I looked around the room for a few seconds before I continued. "But, I did meet someone."

"What's his name?"

"*Her* name is Samantha."

"Oh, yeah? Sam. Does Sam have any female friends?"

"We'll find out soon. We're meeting them once Nirvana is offstage."

"Okay, man. Good deal. You know that I am always down with the ladies."

"Oh, I know it."

"Yep. It's tough being this magnificent."

We stepped back for a while and enjoyed the concert from the fringes of the densely packed crowd in front. Just out of reach of the lunatics. The music was great, but it was just so hard not to dwell on Samantha and seeing her again.

Soon enough we were going through the obligatory encore performance. I always wondered why we bothered with an encore; it was always the same. First, the band wrapped up and left the stage. Second, everyone screamed and begged for more. Finally, the band came out and played again for a little bit. It was so routine, yet everyone around me fed the monster by screaming frantically for more at every show. *What happens when the bands aren't any good,* I thought to myself. *Do people still shout for an encore?*

The place became a little hectic and eclectic as people started to clear out. We made our way to the t-shirts to hang out. There were people buying them left and right, now that the show was over. Seeing that I was preoccupied, Scott went over to buy us a couple of them.

I looked around but didn't see Samantha. The anticipation had been building for a while, but it was really starting to peak and made me a little jittery. Scott looked at me and raised his eyebrows. I shrugged a little bit. I could see he was getting a little restless.

Scott turned toward two girls, one blonde and one brunette, who were standing nearby.

"What are you ladies drinking?" Scott asked them. They were holding plastic cups.

"Water." The blonde replied.

"Water?" Scott repeated. I groaned, but nobody could hear it. He was always doing this kind of stuff. "Might I suggest that you try a Jack and Scott..."

"What?" the blonde asked him, with a quizzical yet amused expression. I could tell that the charm was starting to work on her. The brunette, however, wasn't amused. She whispered in her friend's ear and they scurried away. The blonde looked back over her shoulder and gave Scott a quick smile as they departed.

"Take care, ladies!" Scott called out.

"Nice," I said and laughed.

"Hey...they could sense your hesitation, bro. *That's* why they walked away. Where's your fella at, anyway? Sam's his name, right?"

I looked around again, slowly—didn't want to seem too eager. Then I saw her. My heart may have actually stopped—it was hard to tell—but something definitely wreaked some minor havoc on my senses and motor skills. Something unintelligible came out of my mouth—an attempt at words—that sounded more like a bad Conan the Barbarian imitation.

The brown hair and chestnut eyes struck me again. The smooth, tanned skin. She saw me then, smiled, and I was smitten. I managed to smile back.

"Wow…" Scott said, under his breath. I could see him turn and look at me in the periphery of my vision. "Ah-hah…I see now," he said.

"Hi, Jack." Samantha said. I don't think it was the strange arena lighting…I think she really was glowing.

"Hi, Samantha."

I stared at her dumbly for a moment, with what was probably the grin of an idiot, but I was surprisingly unconcerned.

"Oh! Hey, this is Jackie and this is Raquel," she said, pointing at the two pretty brown-haired girls at her sides.

"And, Scott," I snapped, awakening from my own stupor. "We're roommates." Everyone shook hands all around, but I barely noticed. "Do you want to go somewhere for coffee or something?"

"That'd be great," Samantha replied.

The five of us clicked and the rest of the night was a blur of happiness and discovery for me. I had never met anyone as interesting as Samantha. Or smart—she was studying to be a computer engineer at Rice. For a small town girl, she was out of this world!

I didn't know it at the time, but one day, that girl was going to be my wife.

Chapter 3
Tuesday Afternoon, July 31st, 2012

Ryan's family lived in the same part of Northwest Austin that we did, except they were closer to Lake Travis. I pulled up in front of their home and cut my Land Rover's engine. Sam and I had debated over whether we should fess up the money and go for a Range Rover, but in the end, we traveled the path of the fiscally responsible parents that we wanted to be (mostly). It was easier for Sam...much tougher for me. Electronics and cars were my temptations in this world. But, the Land Rover was still a beautiful vehicle—the nicest I had owned. I got out of my baby, walked up to the front door, and gave it a good knock.

"Hi, Jack!" Ryan's mom, Paula, opened the door and greeted me warmly. She was a fairly happy person, and a little quirky, but always friendly. Her husband, Mark, worked late frequently. He was a big shot at the local law firm that called Dell a client. Mark lived the stories you read about in John Grisham books. He was a friendly guy who kept me laughing because he was always spinning yarns about getting out of the game and just processing tax returns.

"Hey, Paula. How's life?"

"It's good. Come on in and I'll call the boys. They're upstairs playing one of those games where you shoot people and there's blood and all that. You want a drink? I was just about to have a glass of Moscato."

"No, that's fine. I'm tired already. Wine would finish me off."

"Okey-dokey," she chirped, "but, I'm going to go ahead and have some...it's been calling my name all day." The kitchen was off to the left when you entered their home. It meshed well with the large, open floor plan they had downstairs, and the large, showcase windows gave it a bright and airy feel. There was a similarity to our own house—which may be the reason I liked it so much. *After all, it feels like home.* Paula made her way to the bar, which wrapped around about half of the kitchen, and poured herself some wine from the bottle that was already loaded in a bottle cooler. The Martins were good people and we were happy to have them as friends.

"Mark still at work?"

"Oh, of course. But he should be home soon. He says he is going to gradually reduce how much they have their claws in him."

"Yeah, I don't know about that…"

"Me either," she said taking a sip, walking over to the stairs on the other side of the foyer. I followed her and could hear, faintly, the sound of guns and explosions. It was probably *Modern Warfare.* Both boys had asked for it this last year. Jake even said he *needed* it. I had played it with him a few times and had to admit: it was addicting. "Boys! Jake's dad is here!" she called out. She then turned to me and continued her thought, "I think Mark likes what he does more than he lets on. He just doesn't want us to know he likes it that much."

"Ha. Yeah, you're probably right," I told her, and she *was* probably right. Mark was a really smart guy; he was good at what he did. He could never be relegated to preparing tax returns, although I was certain he could excel at anything he tried. I knew all of this, not only from our decade of friendship, but also because he was our lawyer, too. His specialty involved the big companies, but he made an exception for us.

Just then I heard the sound of two sets of feet running across the floor above us. It wasn't loud, but it was hearty. The boys were best friends, full of energy, and always on the hunt for adventure. They rarely sat still for more than a few minutes. My mother had a saying for that: *boys will be boys.* She really over-utilized it for any point she was trying to make about boys, but she was right. Soon they were running down the stairs.

"Hey, Dad!" Jake proclaimed.

"Hey, buddy! Did you have a good day?"

"Yeah, Dad, it was pretty awesome. You know how we roll."

"Indeed. You roll awesomely. Say...it sounds like you're killing people up there. I hope that you're one of the good guys, fighting for freedom, wherever there's trouble..."

"Sure, Dad. We're the good guys." My *G.I. Joe* reference went unrecognized. Even though there had been movie remakes, they seemed to focus on big-movie, blockbuster action as the theme without nostalgic value. I could understand the motive behind that (sales), but it made me a little sad that the days of my youth were quickly becoming ancient history. The G.I. Joe movies were okay, but they didn't feel the same.

"We went to the Apple store today." Jake said.

"Oh, yeah?"

"Ohhh, yeah! The iPad is completely sweet, Dad. We messed around with the new one for a while." Jacob was like me—electronics tugged at the heart and mind—an expensive obsession to have and he was starting early.

"I had to run some errands earlier at the mall," Paula added.

"You mean shopping..."

"Like I was *saying*, I ran some errands...at the *mall*...and the boys had some ice cream and went to the Apple store while we were there."

"Did you tell Mrs. Paula thanks?"

"Duh, Dad, come on," he said, exasperated expression painted across his face.

"Well, tell her again." I prodded him.

"Thank you, Mrs. Martin. What about the iPad, Dad? Birthday?"

"We'll see. Grab your stuff. It's time to boogie." He lifted up his backpack at me and raised his eyebrows. The look said, *Got my stuff, Dad, Duh!* "Paula, thanks for watching this guy." I leaned over to Jake and rubbed his hair. He put his hand on my shoulder and gave me a grin. Except for the occasional sarcastic comment or reply (probably learned from his old man), Jacob was the best kid ever. All the time I thought about what a great little person he had become: honest, smart, funny, and loyal. I pulled him over and hugged him to me a little extra.

Paula finished her wine and set the empty glass on a nearby table. "It was easy. These guys are easy." Truer words never spoken.

~~~~~

To celebrate my last promotion, Samantha, Jacob, and I had taken a two-week vacation to Italy. It was an amazing experience filled with great food and many adventures. The Italians, it seemed to me, led the world in passion. They were passionate about clothing, passionate about their cooking, and beyond passionate when communicating, with explosive and elaborative hand gestures second to none. At least three times, I saw somebody slap their hand on the hood of a car and make lots of grandiose gestures after nearly being run over...they were also passionate drivers.

One of our discoveries was something we (surprisingly) had overlooked in the good old United States: Gnocchi! It was sort of like the 'macaroni and cheese' of Italy—hard not to like—so simple, yet so tasty. Since that trip, Gnocchi found its way to our tabletop at least once a month.

I was about to combine the formaggio sauce with the Gnocchi when I heard the soft electronic *beep* from our front door being opened. If Samantha was wearing flats I would see her quickly, after only a second or two...she'd kick them off and come right to the kitchen. If she were wearing boots, like her Uggs, it took a little longer for her to take them off, and it would be a minute before she came around the corner. I looked up—waiting—watching.

Only a few seconds passed before I saw her. The very air seemed to change density when she entered a room. Even after so many years, it surprised me how beautiful she was, and how she made me feel. It made me smile to myself.

"What?" she asked, coming in, setting her things down on our *keys-and-things* shelf off the foyer. "What are you smiling at?" And, yet, she was smiling, too.

"Well, hello to you, too! I was just thinking about how beautiful you are." I wondered briefly if Samantha ever got tired of hearing me say things like that, or if it wasn't as believable because I had said it so often. I had told her how much I loved her every day of our marriage, because the truth was that I never tired of it, and I always wanted her to know.

"Okay...what do you want now?" she asked, still smiling, and walked over to where I stood in front of the stove.

"I think you know what I want..." I said, standing up and putting my arms around her. I buried my face in that magical place between her hair and neck, and with my nose against the skin of her neck, inhaled deeply. It was the most welcome scent in the world. It made me feel a hundred different things inside, all of them positive in different ways. "Mmm..."

Things were going well for a couple of minutes. Then something in the air changed. Literally.

"Ooh. I think your food's burning."

"Oh, man!" I turned quickly to the stove and stirred my Gnocchi. A few of them had burned to the bottom of the pan, but luckily, everything still looked edible.

Samantha had moved off and was engaged in those little acts of work depressurization I had seen a thousand times since we were married. First she removed her watch. Next, she rubbed her arms briskly a couple of times, up and down, as if there was a chill in the air. Then she moved her hands up to her hair, deftly unfastened something, and brought her hair down. Finally, she lifted her hair back up, looser this time, into a different position. She pushed something into her hair to hold it up and she was done with her body. She looked more comfortable. Now it was time for her things.

She pushed her things aside on our knick-knack table. Cell phone went to the charger. She was the smartest woman I knew, but she could be messy. A small heap of mystery purse stuff remained on the tabletop. It might make it back into her purse and it might not. You never knew.

"I love you," I told her.

"I love you, too." She smiled and walked to the

cabinets, removed three dinner plates, and placed them on the counter. Jacob burst into the room just then.

"Hey, Mom!" Jake had always been a little bit of a mommy's boy, which was fine with us. It was very important to me that Jake cherished his mother. I tried to teach him to extend, to a degree, those feelings to other ladies, as well. In my opinion, ladies comprised the nucleus of society; the core of all that was good in this world began with a woman and her child. I was proud of Jake for being more mature than his friends when it came to relationships with your parents.

"Hey, buddy, come on over." She opened her arms and Jake didn't shy away from the obligatory, daily home-from-work hug that Sam always wanted. That was good. I had noticed that his friends were already rejecting open signs of affection with their mothers. Jake's best friend, Ryan, always said, *"Mohhhm,"* drawing the word out, frowning and wincing, pulling away from his mom if she tried to hug him.

Samantha gave him an extra squeeze at the end of their embrace and rubbed her hand through his hair. Jake's appearance was a great combination of the two of us. Some people thought Jake looked like me; some people thought Jake looked like his mom. Really, it was both. I loved that.

"Clean up, dude. It's Gnocchi night."

"Awesome. Are we going to have salad? With Olive Garden dressing?" he asked. Ever since we discovered last year that Olive Garden bottled their dressing and sold it, we had become addicted, and picked up a bottle or two every visit.

"Sure, hon. I'll make it. You just wash the boy-grime off your hands." Samantha walked over to the refrigerator and began to pull out the makings for a quick salad. Jacob cleaned his hands, then finished setting up the table for dinner. It all came together naturally and I thought to myself for the billionth time that my family was unbeatable, unstoppable, and the best ever.

"What's gonna work..." I said, and then my wife and I said in unison, *"Teamwork!"*

"Okay, Dad. Enough of that," Jake replied.

"Dude, just five years ago you were singing along with the *Wonder Pets*. I know you remember the words."

"Maybe, Dad. But, they're not cool when you're almost 11 years old." He had a point, but that didn't mean that I had to surrender gracefully to his getting older.

We settled into dinner at the table adjacent to the kitchen. We had a formal dining room, but it rarely saw any action. It's funny how things like that happen…we always used our little breakfast nook instead of the dining room. It was comfortable and fun. I enjoyed it so much—our meals together—the three of us being so close to one another.

I poked at my food and thought about my own childhood. My mom tried to be the uniting force in our world, but there were some things that she just couldn't do without a husband that's actively engaged with his kids. That was especially true before the money came in, and she had to work just so that we could scrape by each month. Even so, to a large degree, things were beyond her control and would never change.

Chapter 4
1983

I was in my room with the door closed. There was an epic struggle ensuing; it might determine the fate of the world.

"Give up Storm Shadow…there are two of us. You can't win." I had two G.I. Joe action figures, Duke and Gung Ho, poised for battle with Storm Shadow, the evil Cobra's ninja assassin, clad in white.

Storm Shadow laughed as I moved him toward Duke. "Duke, you were never very smart. I'm going to have to take you down." With what I imagined was movement at lightning speed, I thrust Storm Shadow at Duke with a terrific roundhouse kick. Duke went down, as forewarned by Storm Shadow. Gung Ho stepped in and took his place, but he wasn't as confident as before and it was obvious.

"Storm Shadow," he reasoned, "why are you doing this? Join us. Be one of the good guys." Storm Shadow appeared to consider it, but then started laughing. He drew his sword and once more a battle raged.

"Jacky! Dinner time!" my mom called out.

Man, just when things were getting good! I set the G.I. Joes I had in my hands off to the side and ran into the living room. My sister was watching *Charlie Brown* on the television. She was sitting right in front of the television, head tilted back at a ridiculous angle so that she could see the picture.

"Hey, why didn't you tell me that was on?" I asked her.

"Well, I didn't think you cared. You said last time that you didn't like *Charlie Brown* anymore." She said this in a matter-of-fact tone.

I walked over and lightly pinched the volume-and-power knob on the TV between my fingers and raised my eyebrows. "What if I turn it off?"

She assessed the situation with a calm demeanor that

was beyond her years and then smiled. It almost seemed like she felt sorry for me. "I'm sorry I didn't tell you, Jack. You can turn it off if you want." She looked at me with nothing but honesty in her face. I looked at her for a second and then let go of the knob.

"I'm just kidding, Sis." Just like that, she contained the mischief that was brewing. "You're going to hurt your neck, sitting that close to the tee-vee," I added.

Dutifully, Katie stood up and moved back a few feet. She didn't have any problems seeing the television. It was simply one of her little peccadillos to scoot closer, closer, and closer, to the television whenever she was engrossed in a program. My mom thought it was due to her level of excitement, that it was an attempt by Katie to get so close that she would actually feel like she was inside the television show.

Our house was small—very small—and our mom was visible in the kitchen through an opening behind and above the couch. She smiled at us over the countertop and said, "Come on guys...dinner's ready." Katie and I bolted to the dining room where a pleasant surprise awaited us.

"Mac and cheese!" Katie squealed. Macaroni was a favorite of the Leonard kids. And, in addition to macaroni and cheese, were fried pork chops.

"Hey, Katie...what do you call a pig that knows karate?" I asked my sister.

"What?"

"A pork chop!" I replied. We all giggled and moved toward our usual spots.

I was pretty excited—it was one of my favorite meals from my mother's repertoire. Except, when I sat down, I noticed that there was no plate set out for my dad. This wasn't unusual.

"Is Dad going to have dinner with us?" I asked. I looked around for signs that he might be home: truck keys on the bar, or newspaper on the chair. I didn't see any.

"I don't think so, honey," Mom replied, giving me one of

those sad looks that reveal the depth of emotion mothers have for their children. Our eyes met briefly, but I looked away. I was embarrassed. Mine was a family where boys didn't show weakness. Even at eight years of age, I had figured that out.

"Okay. He must be working late," I said even though I knew it was *far* from the truth; however, it was important to me that Katie be given the impression that Dad would be here if he weren't *obligated* to be somewhere else.

I didn't know it all (again, eight years old), but I knew at least some of what my father did every night. There was rarely an evening when he didn't smell like beer; there were an equally few number of days when he was sober.

He wasn't an angry drunk. He was actually sort of silly. Overly friendly and easygoing. If he came home while I was awake he would get involved in whatever I was doing. He would sort of stumble and drop down to the floor next to me and grab my G.I. Joe guys, intuitively take my lead, and join into the battle that was raging. There were a few times when he stayed there with me the rest of the night, until I was done playing, however long that might be. It was like he transformed into a child himself when he played with me like that. I loved it.

So, it was very hard to understand why he couldn't be home with us. Or, why he *wouldn't* be home with us. Why did he have to *go* somewhere else...*be* with other people? I felt like he loved me (when I saw him), but I just figured that he must love something, or someone, more than us. Most of the dads I knew were home with their family at dinnertime.

But my dad wasn't most dads...*he was my dad*.

Some nights when he wasn't home, I felt it worse than others. The pain, I mean. I kept those times from my mom because I didn't want her to worry about me. I kept it from everyone else because I didn't want anyone to think I was weak or a baby. But sometimes, at the end of the night, I quietly let the tears fall from my eyes until I fell asleep under a cloak of sadness.

Chapter 5
Thursday Morning, August 2nd, 2012

Thursdays were my early day; the light, plucky sound of the xylophone came on at 4 am, prodding me into consciousness. I ran or biked 3-5 days a week, but Thursday was my slow, peaceful run. I stole some extra time to contemplate all the little things in my life.

Or, I went the opposite direction, didn't think about anything, and just enjoyed the view. Either way, it was another figurative Zen place for me.

The sound of the xylophone alarm on my iPhone was peaceful. That's not something I say lightly, some casual remark, without due consideration. My entire life I've hated the sound of alarms: passionately. In high school the sound of my alarm clock triggered an actual stomachache most mornings. In college those alarm-clock-stomachaches continued—frequently joined by a surly companion—the headache. Of course, the booze may have had something to do with that.

In a perfect world I would awaken naturally. No buzzing, beeping, radio static, or music. One moment eyes closed, the next moment open—nothing else—followed by as much time in bed as needed before rising. But, until that day was here, I had to hand it to the minions over at Apple—the xylophone tone was a pleasant and reasonable sound, for an alarm.

I didn't want to wake Samantha, so I quickly undocked my iPhone from the alarm clock stereo and silenced it. I swung my feet to the floor, sat on my side of the bed, and listened for a moment. Comingling with the soft swish of our ceiling fan was my wife's breathing. It was slow and steady. She was still asleep.

I stood up and padded over to our closet. I felt lucid and loose and knew instinctively that I was going to have a great run. I didn't always know this, but now and then I felt completely in tune and unstoppable. I felt like that now.

A few moments later, I closed our front door, tucked my key into the strange little zipper pocket on the back of my shorts, and stretched for a few minutes. Our street was peaceful. It was gray outside, but not dark, and cool. I thought back to a basic meteorology course I had taken in college. We had learned that the period of time from when you begin to see light outside, but before the sun actually crests the horizon, was called Beginning Morning Nautical Twilight or B-M-N-T. This was important for a couple of reasons, I think, but all I could remember was that it was also the time of day that fog was most likely to form. *Sunrise surprise* they called it.

A light mist kissed the edges of the neighborhood, trying to creep in further, but held at bay by some invisible force. *One point for the meteorology professor*, I thought.

I set the app on my iPhone to map and track both my path and run-times. It still amazed me that that was possible. I remembered getting my mom to drive me along running routes in middle school, to measure them, so that I could estimate my pace.

I finished stretching and moved quickly to the road. I chose a path that would gradually wind through my neighborhood, take me uphill, and then loop to the east before coming back. It was going to be about eight miles—a little farther than normal—but I didn't want to let the positive energy go to waste.

Things were quiet this time of day and in this part of town. I passed another runner going the opposite direction—a lanky female with a long stride. We had passed each other before in the silence before sunrise. The only pleasantries we exchanged were a simple smile and the lifting of a hand.

The blocks passed quickly. I vacillated between sidewalk and road, as necessary, like the pendulum of a clock. I listened to my music, and contemplated my surroundings in some vague way while, periodically, images of Sam and Jake flitted through my mind.

Near the last mile of my route I clicked my iPhone and turned off the music so that I could listen to the natural sounds around me. It was a very personal part of my morning running routine. I listened to, and felt, my breathing. I was in the zone, but even so, I was breathing hard. I was pushing it. It could have been real, or my imagination, but I was pretty certain I could feel the beating of my heart. It was rhythmic…*thump-thump*, pause, *thump-thump*, pause.

I could also hear the sound of my running shoes striking the pavement—*thap, thap, thap*—and the sounds coalesced into a comforting and friendly companion. Samantha had once pointed out a Nike commercial and said that it reminded her of me. The man in the advertisement woke up early, before daylight, and went running. The sound of his footsteps were the only thing you could hear in the morning darkness as he made his peace in the world.

I liked that.

Sometimes, I felt like my life was nearly perfect. My wife and son were amazing—there were no better people in existence. I was one of those rare guys that actually *liked* his job—heaven help the people that didn't—I couldn't imagine devoting 25% of my life to something that I didn't enjoy.

Yeah, I concluded, *I do have it all. Everything I ever wanted.*

I was nearly home. I sped up and gave it everything, legs pumping, lungs burning, as I ran the last few blocks. I pushed my body to its limits. I felt like a piston firing, firing, firing, as I ran. I was like a fluid, in motion, perfectly synchronized with everything in my environment. It was like the scene in *Rocky II*, when Rocky is training for his rematch with Apollo Creed and he's running through the streets of Philadelphia and most of the city is running behind him. But he outruns them. That's how I felt. *Minus the city full of people running behind me.*

I crossed the imaginary plane extending from my front door to the street—my unofficial finish line—and dropped my speed to a slow jog. The slow jog turned into a fast amble and eventually slowed to a moderate walking pace. My breathing was a little ragged again. I had pushed hard, but it felt great.

Did I push that hard in football? I wondered. *Yeah, I did,* I answered myself quickly. I pushed much harder in football, but it was hard to compare the two because they were different.

Two-a-days were the perfect example. We had football practice twice each day, Monday through Saturday, for the last two weeks before summer ended and school began.

It was brutal.

Texas in the summer is ridiculously humid when you're sitting still. Add personal protective equipment and pads, sprints, calisthenics, screaming coaches, patterns, and all the rest into the equation, and a hot and humid Texas summer quickly became Hades.

We had all tossed our cookies at least once during two-a-days. Most guys emptied their stomachs a few times before they got back into the rhythm. And those were the guys that had worked out during the summer.

The guys that didn't, paid for it. There were always a couple of dudes that messed around all summer and lost their conditioning. They drank too much beer; they stayed up all night. They made the mistake of thinking that they could fake it through practices.

The coaches were like slacker bloodhounds. They sniffed and sniffed until they picked up the scent. When they picked up that malodorous swamp-like mixture of exhaustion, fear, and cheap wine on those guys, they pursued their prey mercilessly. They drilled them, and drilled them, and drilled them. If you weren't so damned tired yourself, you'd feel bad for them, but you were just too tired and there were too many coaches.

Yeah...we pushed ourselves hard back then. That's just how it was, and we all accepted it. We did it because we wanted to be part of a group that not many people could be a part of. We considered ourselves elite; in some ways we were right.

We were also young. It's a lot easier to push yourself to the limits in your youth. A 15-year-old body recovers more quickly than a 37-year-old body. That's just life.

I walked around the streets for a few minutes to let that 37-year-old body of mine cool down. The sun was just poking up above the horizon, a brilliant sliver of heat and life, giving Austin a good morning kiss.

When I reached our front yard, I dropped down onto the grass, and closed my eyes. I was feeling good and enjoying being lost in my thoughts. Through my adulthood I had consistently, year by year, become more introspective. It was really and truly a shame to have to break that profound reverie, that time spent looking inward, for work. I felt that I was close to getting key pieces of the Jack Leonard puzzle dropped into place.

I thought about all those years of football: peewee, middle school, and high school. I reasoned that I was able to push myself as hard as I did *now* because I had learned how to push myself so hard *then*.

It was always me and Scott back then, I reflected, *pushing through things together*. I felt so relaxed laying there in the yard. It felt like I was floating…or drifting…

"Jack, are you okay?"

My eyes flickered open and I sat up.

"Jack, you're going to be late for work," Samantha called. She was in the doorway in pajama pants and a t-shirt. I loved it when she dressed like that.

I jumped up and trotted over to her: "Thanks, honey."

"You're welcome. What were you doing out there?" she asked, picking bits of grass off my back. "Wow, you're covered in dew…how long were you laying there?"

"I don't know. I guess I just got lost in my own head. I was thinking about all those years I played football. *We* played football. Scott and I were always a team, you know? Anyway…"

"Hmm…interesting. I'm going back to bed for a few minutes."

"Okay. Love you."

"Love you, too." She said as she walked down the hallway back to bed.

Chapter 6
1990

Scott and I were in the weight room adjacent to our high school football field. We were *encouraged* to work out after practice, which really meant that those of us starting in our position had better be working out. If we didn't, Coach Johnson would find a not-so-subtle way of working us harder in practice.

The weight room was fairly state-of-the-art—it was Texas football, after all—and it had everything you needed to work out the entire body. Plus, it was never crowded. The football, baseball, and basketball coaches had oversight of gym use and they restricted it to people who were involved in the sports that they coached. It wasn't a fair system, but again, Texas likes its football players.

"Hey, brother, can you slap another 25-pound plate on that side?" Scott asked. Like most young guys, we were obsessed with bench presses and were taking turns on the flat bench. I grabbed a 25-pound plate and added it to one side while he added one to the other side.

"That's a little heavy, Scott. Are you ready for that?"

"Jack, you know that when you're lifting...when you're going heavy...more plates equals more dates."

I chuckled at one of the bad jokes that had bounced around the weight room the past year and added some more: "That's right. Gettin' the cuts for the sluts...the hams for the mams."

Scott laughed, laid down on the bench, and shimmied up under the Olympic bar. "The guy with the biggest chest and bi's gets the ladies that show the breasts and thighs," he added. I laughed again, because as lame as they were, the jokes never got old to me.

I stepped onto the platform behind the bench to give

Scott a spot. He rubbed his hands together and I did a quick tally of the weights as he found the right placement for his hands on the bar. It was going to be a personal record for him. Neither of us said anything as he grasped the bar and I guided it out and over him. Talking about it might jinx it. Go with it like it's normal stuff.

Scott lowered the weight down and his already red complexion went a shade darker. The bar tapped his chest and he raised it as he exhaled. "One," I said, "...now give me another."

Scott lowered the bar again, tapped off the chest, and pressed it back up. I could see that he was pushing it. "Two...I know you have one more. Give me one more."

Scott lowered the bar a third time, tapped off the chest, and pressed it back up. I could see that he was drained as his arms reached almost full extension and I was there to grab the bar and guide it back into place. The weights gave a satisfying *clink!* when the bar was back in position.

Now that it was over, it was okay to talk about it: "Holy crap, brother, you put up some serious weight that time...three reps!"

"Whew...yeah..." he agreed, standing up, shaking it off while I removed the 25-pound plates for my own set.

"Definitely going to get some *dates* with that lift." I said, laughing.

He was drinking some water when I said it and started choking, which made me laugh even harder.

"You're going to pay for that, Redneck. Some day when you least expect it."

"Oh, okay, tough guy," I said, then added in my best Rocky Balboa versus Mr. T. voice: "You ain't so bad! You ain't so bad!"

We continued working out and talking just like we always did. Football and girls were the primary ingredients of our gym conversations, along with a healthy smattering of bad jokes. Bad jokes were omnipresent in our universe.

48

"Dude, I think we're picking up barbecue tonight for dinner."

"Oh, I forgot to tell you…my mom wants to go out to eat tonight…she's gonna pick me up today."

"What's the occasion?" I asked. Scott usually caught a ride home with me and my mom. His mom regularly worked late, and of course, his dad was in absentia.

"I think there's a guy she wants me to meet."

"Whoa, a guy? Your mom has a beau that she wants you to meet?"

"Yeah."

"Weird."

"Tell me about it."

"Weird."

"You said that already."

"I guess I did." I was at a loss for words. Scott's mother really didn't get involved with men. Actually, now that I thought about it, I wasn't sure that I had ever heard of her going on dates or being involved with suitors…at least not that she let on to us about. If she did, it was kept under wraps from me, and probably Scott, too.

"I know the guy. They work together."

"Oh, yeah?"

"Yeah. He seems alright. I guess I won't pull any funny stuff or try to embarrass my mom." I could see that he was in good humor again.

We finished up our workout and went outside with a few of the other freshmen players, to wait for parental units to pick us up. Parker Jones, who could never sit still, immediately got out his hacky sack and started doing his thing with it.

"Why do you always kick that thing around, Parker?" Big John Klein, already over six feet tall, asked him. Everyone else called Parker Jones by his last name because he hated *Parker* for some reason.

Jason Kelso: "It's fun, John…get off his back."

"Don't make me angry, Jason. You won't like

me...when I'm angry." John said this in sort of a joking way, but also with an edge underneath the surface. He was a really great guy, but he was also really good at being a big, dumb jock.

"It's fun, Hulk. It's just fun."

John looked pleased to be called Hulk...he was very proud of his size. Jones was a pretty cool character—I always gave him that—he had diffused the situation without being overbearing or aggressive. We were a pretty cocky group of guys and it wasn't easy to quell these egos. But he had done it swiftly, effortlessly.

I didn't know it at the time, but I would be playing ball with most of these same guys through my final year in high school.

We continued to joke around as, one by one, parents and older siblings pulled up. Bags full of gear and backpacks were piled into the backs of trucks and vans, boys jumped in, and then they were gone.

My mom was always punctual about picking Scott and me up from football practice. We might find her chatting with other mothers, if they were early, or we ran late. Today, however, I found myself alone after Big John's little, tiny mother picked him up. She drove a gigantic Chevy Suburban and scattered pebbles when she pulled out of the lot quickly.

I was considering walking, or calling someone for a ride, when I saw my father's truck. Actually, I *heard* him before I *saw* him: the sound of country music announced his arrival. I didn't know the song, but I recognized George Strait (one of Dad's fave-o-right singers).

I turned my head and there he was, windows down, cowboy hat on, one elbow poked out over the windowsill, while his fingers tapped the window frame. *Pure Billy Leonard*, I thought.

As I watched, the truck turned into the parking lot, narrowly missing the curb. To the untrained eye it might look like nothing. It wasn't a radical miscalculation, just a little swerve at the last second. But the first thing that crossed my mind was that my dad had been drinking. I was glad that my friends weren't around to see this.

He pulled up and stopped beside me: "Hey, hop in buddy."

I grabbed my stuff and tossed it into the bed of the truck. I noticed his range bag in the corner...he'd been at the firing range at some point. As I got into his truck, I noted the innocuous looking sports drink container between his legs. My dad didn't drink sports drinks.

"Hey, Dad..."

"Yeah, bud..."

"Where's Mom?"

"She had some things to do...asked me to come getcha. Shut the door."

I hesitated. I didn't ride with my dad that much anymore. My mother chauffeured us everywhere we wanted to go. But...my dad had no qualms driving after a few beers. If he considered himself *drunk*, he wouldn't drive, but he rarely considered himself *drunk*. He classified his usual state of being as *feelin' good*. If he had had any moral dilemmas with drinking and driving, he would never have been able to drive; he was always drinking a little bit. He was *feelin' good* most of his waking hours.

My dad could see my hesitation and intuitively (or through experience with my mom) knew what it was about. His brows furrowed a little bit and his eyes got squinty like they did when he was annoyed. It was a look usually reserved for political discussions.

"Come on, Jack. Jump in."

"Hey, Dad...how about you let me drive? It's almost time for me to get my license anyway..."

He saw through me pretty easily. I will give my father this: he was the highest functioning alcoholic you'd ever meet. "Get in, Jack. Don't act like your mother." He was brusque, and annoyed, but he rarely got really *angry*. Just annoyed. Angry was reserved for those highly isolated moments when he got *really* sauced.

He was my dad and I loved him. I disagreed with him—*this was wrong*—but I was still a kid. So I got in the truck.

Chapter 7
Saturday & Sunday, August 4th & 5th, 2012

When we pulled into the large u-shaped driveway at my parents' house, I saw Katie's SUV, and my already good mood soared. "Uh-oh, Jake...looks like Aunt Katie and Uncle Mike beat us here."

"Well, Dad, that's because we didn't leave yesterday like we could have."

"It was late, dudeski."

"Dad..." he said, dissenting, explaining with a single word the depth of his disapproval for leaving a day later than we could have. I could see him eyeballing me in the rearview mirror.

"Oh, yeah?"

"Yeah."

"You're right, man. We could have left last night. But, I was tired. Mom was tired. Had to play it safe and keep it safe."

"Dad's right." Samantha chimed in. "Best to play it safe. We're here now and you'll be playing with your cousins in no time. Love you, bud."

"Love you, Mom. Love you, too, Dad."

"Thank you, thank you very much." I said in a bad Elvis imitation.

The front door burst open as we came to a stop behind the silver Toyota Sequoia. Katie's kids, Mike Jr. and Miranda, bore down on us in typical excited-kid fashion—like tiny, clumsy heat-seeking missiles with limbs. "Jake! Jake!" they shouted.

Jake jumped out and the three kids immediately tumbled around in the grass together. Jake was a little older, but they all got along...like peas and carrots, as Forrest Gump would say.

"Sis!" I bellowed when Katie came jogging outside. I

ran over and picked her up for a quick bear-hug and put her down again. Samantha, Mike, and my parents were there moments later, and there was a round of hugs all around.

"How was the drive?" my dad asked. It was always the first thing he said. He was getting older—set in his ways—predictable. Sometimes predictable is good, like slipping on your favorite shoes; you know exactly how they'll fit.

"Drive was good, Dad. Not too much traffic, except around here, in Houston. But not bad."

"Good. We're glad you all could come down again before school."

"Yes," Mom chimed in, beaming, "it's so nice to have my kids and my beautiful grandkids here again!" She smiled, leaned forward, and applied a generous hug to Jake when the kids worked their way over to us.

I looked around at everyone and smiled. Billy gave Jake a playful punch to the shoulder. Samantha leaned down, said something to Miranda, who giggled, and replied excitedly. Mike gave Jake a high-five. Katie tousled Mike Jr.'s hair. My mother, all the while, stood watching, soaking it up greedily, like a desert flower in the rain.

It didn't matter that I had my own family and owned my own house; this would always be my home. It was good to be home.

We piled inside and made our way to the kitchen and living room. This was where everyone always congregated. It was an open floor design with a kitchen and breakfast area that opened up to the main living area. My mother began busily taking drink orders and handing out sodas while everyone talked at once.

"Kids are looking forward to school."

"Do you think A&M has a chance this year?"

"The heat has just been unbearable this summer."

"*The Dark Knight Rises* was awesome!"

"So awful about the shootings in Colorado—the country seems to be ripe with animals these days."

I talked, I listened, and I relaxed. I enjoyed the ruckus of my family.

Eventually, the kids ran off to play, and our many separate conversations converged into one that we all participated in.

"Mike, Samantha…do you mind if I steal Katie and Jack for some range time? I've got a spot reserved. It starts soon."

"I don't know, Dad…" I started to protest. We *had* just arrived and I didn't want to bail on Sam so soon. I looked at her.

"That's fine," she smiled. "Go have fun."

"You sure?" I asked.

"Of course."

"Okay." I looked at my dad. "Sounds fun. It's been a while since I fired off some rounds."

"I'll grab the pistols…they're just sitting in the safe, ready to go. Katie Bird, are you up for it?"

"Sure, Dad. Mike can hang out with Mom and Samantha." She raised her voice, "Isn't that right, Mike?"

"Yes, dear. Mike can hang out with Mom and Samantha," Mike replied, which made me laugh. He wasn't an athletic guy, but he was intelligent and funny. Most importantly, he doted on Kaitlyn and was a good father. This was important for Mike's health and wellbeing since I could be overprotective of my sister.

My dad wandered off to his office, where he had a large safe that housed a variety of pistols, rifles, and shotguns. I found Jake, little Mike, and Miranda all laughing and giggling in the living room.

"What's so funny, guys?"

"Miranda farted, Dad," Jake replied, doubling over with fresh laughter.

I shook my head. "Alright. Well, Aunt Katie and I are going out with Grandpa for a little bit, so give me a big hug." Jake leapt from the chair and complied. He was a good little man. "Take care of your mom while I'm gone."

"Sure thing, Dad," he said.

I walked back to the kitchen and joined Katie just as my dad came in with his range bag. We walked through the kitchen, then the adjoining laundry room, and into the garage.

"Whoa! Dad—you bought a new truck? And a Ford, at that!" I exclaimed, unable to contain my surprise. "Man, look at this...a SuperCrew, 4-door F250. Let me repeat myself: a *Ford*. My whole life you wouldn't acknowledge any truck that wasn't a Dodge."

Katie laughed. "He's right, Dad. What gives? Are you having some sort of mid-...*errr*...late-life crisis?"

"Ha, ha. Okay, you two, very funny."

"Seriously, Dad. Umm, this is interesting...very interesting—"

"Jack, you know, I just drove by it the other day and saw it and I liked it. I figured, what the hell? Plus, it's still an American truck, that's what's really important." He opened up the rear door on the driver's side and slid his bag in. Katie offered up the front seat to me, just like old times, and she and I got into the cab while my dad grabbed something from the spare refrigerator in the garage. I saw him emptying a can into a sports bottle.

"Smells great in here—I love the smell of new cars." Katie cooed.

"Totally, Sis. Me, too."

My dad hit the garage door opener and jumped in the driver's seat. He slipped the sports bottle between his legs as sunlight poured into the opening garage. It felt completely familiar to me, but I didn't really know why.

Then it hit me. A terrible flashback to my younger years. Dad used to always have a beer between his legs, everywhere we went. He'd carry them in one of those cheap, foam koozies.

"Man, Dad, are you serious?"

He jumped a little and turned to me with his brows furrowed. "What?" he snapped.

"That's not beer, is it, Dad? Are you still drinking and driving?"

"Jack, come on, it's just a little bit—"

"Dad, it's 2012," Katie cut him off. "You can't be serious."

"Come on, you two. I thought we left your mom inside the house," he said in a snarky tone.

"Okay, Dad. Here's the deal. I'll drive or Katie can drive. That's the only way I'm going," I told him.

He looked at me disapprovingly and tried to stare me down for a few seconds, but then shook his head, and a small smile lifted the corners of his mouth. "Fine, Jack. You drive. I drink."

I tried not to let the shock show on my face. My father was classically one of the most bull-headed people that I had ever met. For him to back down from this, or anything else, was like having an earthquake in College Station.

Billy jumped out of the driver's seat and we both circled to the rear of the truck. I was a little unnerved by this change of events. Was it a change of heart? Wisdom in his old age? No telling.

We stopped at the tailgate and my dad's smile was broad and genuine. He gave me a quick man-hug, clapped me on the back, and tousled my hair. My confusion left Earth and entered the stratosphere over the Gulf Coast area.

We jumped into our new seats; I put her in gear, and backed down the driveway. My dad was still smiling. I looked in the rearview mirror and Katie was smiling. I shook my head and smiled to myself, too. It almost felt like my father had granted me a knighthood or crowned me king. *I crown thee Jack, knight of East Texas, keeper of peace, and enforcer of sober driving.* It was weird. Good, but weird.

"I love y'all," Dad said to us.

"Love you too, Dad," Katie and I replied, nearly in unison.

Then we all laughed even though, maybe, we shouldn't

have been laughing. I think that families start out, most of the time, with unconditional acceptance of one another. That acceptance starts in childhood and continues into adulthood.

Somewhere in there, between childhood and adulthood, the ability to distinguish right versus wrong is born.

While awareness of right and wrong is meaningful and guides people in lifelong decision-making, it's never truly black and white. The definition of right and wrong differs by location, family, or any of a number of variables. Beliefs evolve over time. There are endless shades of gray.

Can a child be expected to accurately sift through it all, and apply the same standards to his own parents that he would a complete stranger, especially if he doesn't see concrete consequences for the wrongdoing? Not to mention, inherently, a child assumes that their parent is making the right decision. *That's my dad—he does what's right.* How does a child learn what is right or wrong if not from his parents' actions?

They say that it takes 21 days of performing an action to make it a habit. What does that action become after a year? What about after 21 years? I think it's beyond a habit by then...it's who you are. Everyone in my family had verbally chastised my father through the years about his drinking. But that never went far and he never changed his habits.

Even though you stop being a kid, and you grow into adulthood, your mom is still your mom and your dad is still your dad. These were the thoughts going through my mind as we drove off to fire guns with my father while he was drinking.

I know that sounds awful. I throw myself on the mercy of the court. I'm a child not going against his father...a child who had witnessed these same things his entire life without any *real* harm coming to anyone.

I suppose that I was accepting it subconsciously...just as I had all the years before...even though I knew it wasn't right. But that was okay. This time I had won a battle, which over time, could change the tide of a war.

This time he let me drive.

~~~~~

My internal alarm clock woke me up unnecessarily early the next day, so I tramped to the front of the house to check on the kids, and to see what was in the kitchen to munch on. Jacob and his cousins had opted to camp out in the living room in sleeping bags. I had no doubt that they stayed up way too late. They had actually wanted to stay out in the pool house, and I probably would have let them, but both Sam and Katie had dropped the hammer quickly on that idea: *too young*, they said.

"Mornin', Jack," my dad said when I entered the kitchen. He sounded chipper...

(*surprisingly lucid*)

...and was seated at the table reading the newspaper.

"Hey, Dad. Have you looked in on the kids?" I looked in the cabinet and found cereal I hadn't tried before—Special K Vanilla Almond—and poured myself a bowl.

"Yeah, they're doing fine. All breathing," he replied, flipping to the next page.

"You know, Dad, you can get the newspaper delivered to your computer now...or your phone."

"Sure, but I like the way the pages feel in my hands. All these gadgets are just silly."

I smiled to myself as I poured milk over my cereal. "Okay, Tyrannosaurus Billy. Save a tree—read digitally."

"Very funny, wise guy."

I joined him at the table and plunged into my cereal. It was delicious. I had trouble remembering to breathe as I tore into it.

"I hope you left some...it's your mom's...she's very protective of it. All part of one of her new diets." My mom religiously tried all the new diet crazes when they hit the streets. She was fit without them. I think it was more of a hobby-turned-obsession for her.

"Actually, Dad, there are three boxes. Mom's

prepared."

"Good...good."

"Good morning, Leonard men!" Katie said as she popped into the kitchen.

"Hey, Katie," I greeted her.

"Katie Bug!" Dad said. He had been calling her variations of that for as long as I could remember. Katie Bug, Katie Bird, and at the pool: Katie Fish.

"I'm going to go sneak a peek at the munchkins," she said, disappearing into the other room. She came back as I lifted my bowl to finish the remaining milk. I tried not to, but slurped a little.

"Piggy," she said.

"Hey, I'm a growing boy..." I told her, repeating a phrase I had heard applied to pretty much every young boy I had ever met.

"Looks like the Olympics are moving right along," my dad said. "The U.S. is going to end up with a lot of medals this year."

"You mean they decided to go ahead with the Olympics despite Mitt the Twit's warnings?" Katie asked in a joking, yet sarcastic, way. She was a staunch Democrat while my father was a staunch Republican. I was staunchly non-political. Election time often left me grimacing. The urge to hide away from my politically motivated, fireball friends was always a threat.

"Oh, Katie. We were starting off so well..." my dad replied. I waited for it, but there weren't any additional derisive comments. *Could my father be sick? Was he sick...is there a doctor in the house?*

"Well, frankly, I'm shocked at the both of you..." I said. "Dad...no lectures on how we'll all be speaking Chinese soon? Katie...nothing about the we-only-care-about-money politics of the Republicans? Guns? Health Care...nothing?"

My dad's newspaper crinkled as he looked over the top. He gave me a wink.

"I don't think that Dad wants to start something he can't win. Right, Daddy?"

"Sure, sugarplum. Whatever you say," he replied as she gave him a quick hug. She had tried to wake the sleeping bear but failed: he would continue his hibernation. It was the same tactic he had employed more and more with Mom through the years, I had noticed. The bear was still in there somewhere, but the winters were getting longer, and he slept instead of getting grumpy.

"Hey, do you guys want to go to the Schlitterbahn today?"

"Are you serious? Wow, Dad...that's not usually your kind of place." I said.

"Well, you're right, but I got some free passes...hate for them to go to waste."

"Great, Dad!" Katie's ebullient personality was fun to watch. She was one of those rare gems, almost always in a good mood, and always ready for something she considered fun. "We're going to drive back home tonight since Mike has to work early tomorrow, but I'm sure he won't mind."

"Well, let's get those kids up and get going then!" he exclaimed. He stood up, tossed the paper on the table, and strolled into the living room. Katie and I looked at each other in mild shock. "Wake up, wake up, wake up, little monkeys! It's time to go to the waterpark!"

Within minutes the house was a beehive, buzzing with activity.

Samantha: "Good morning, everybody."

Katie, the cheer monger: "Good morning!"

My dad, with the slightest twang: "Mornin'."

Samantha gave me a quick kiss then popped into the kitchen and started eggs for the kids who were already making a ruckus in the living room. Seconds later they appeared next to us, talking animatedly.

"I just don't understand why you watch it," Jake was saying.

"It's an awesome show," Miranda replied.

"Yeah, but it's ridiculous to think that nobody can tell that Hannah Montana is Miley Cyrus. They look *exactly* the same except for blonde hair."

"It's still awesome." Miranda didn't budge.

My mom was the next one to come in. A chorus of 'good mornings' from her grandkids met her loudly and she was soon hugging them and smiling.

"Hey, Mom…hope you don't mind that I had a bowl of your cereal." I told her.

"Of course not, dear."

I looked over at my dad. He rolled his eyes.

I smiled broadly: "Thanks, Mom."

Mike was the last one to make an entrance. It was obvious right away that he was not a morning person. He winced a little bit as everyone fired greetings at him and tried to force a friendly smile to the surface of his face. He wasn't very successful: it looked like a grimace. He immediately went for the coffee pot and got it going.

Considering the various ages and varying degrees of enthusiasm of all parties, I was pleasantly surprised when we were caravanning out to Galveston just an hour later. We settled into two vehicles: my father's truck and our Land Rover. I drove because I loved my vehicle that much. I never wanted to *not* drive it. I couldn't bear to think of it sitting all by its lonesome in the driveway. You can spend a lifetime driving crappy vehicles and never stumble on a good one, but it happened to me, so I made the best out of each opportunity.

My dad drove (probably) because it was another one of the un-verbalized 'man rules' that he followed. He absolutely hated to be a passenger in any vehicle. He also didn't like driving vehicles that weren't trucks. That's probably a Texas stereotype of some sort…one that he qualified for. Mom, Katie and Mike rode with him; we had Mike Jr. and Miranda.

"Sam…I bet one of the reasons my dad bought a 4-door truck was to avoid driving my mom's car *and* to avoid riding in somebody else's."

"Probably."

"He's a funny old Texas coot, isn't he?"

"Stop being so picky, Jack, he's just getting a little older and more set in his ways. Just like you, I could add...you're already getting set in your ways," she said, grinning. "And old. Almost forty! I'm going to be married to an old man."

"Alright, alright."

~~~~~

The day was a huge success. The kids *and* the adults had an amazing time.

My favorite parts of the day were our lazy rides around the park on the Kristal River. The adults grabbed inner tubes, pairing off in couples, relaxing as the current moved us around the waterpark. Well, relaxing as much as you can with three kids splashing and swimming and jumping on your head anyway. Samantha and I just kicked back and chatted and enjoyed being with family.

Even though he was only eleven (almost), I noticed, with no small amount of pride, what a powerful swimmer Jacob was becoming...and already was. He spent chunks of his day playing the gentleman guardian role with his younger cousins. In-between those moments of chivalry, well, it was standard 10-year-old horseplay.

"Jake is so totally going to dominate this year on the swim team," I told Samantha.

"Yes." I could see the pride behind her smile—she was just better at hiding it.

"I wouldn't doubt it if he wins in his age group and division." I looked at Sam and gave her an exaggerated head nod and wink. "Just like his old man...extra manly and tough."

She pulled her sunglasses down over her eyes, smiling, and leaned back without a word. In a way, for women, marriage was like an extended babysitting gig. The woman was committing herself to coddling and watching over a grown man for the rest of her life. I knew that, which I think made me a little bit ahead of the pack. Heck, I knew how lucky I was!

"Dad! Dad, can I ride that?" Jake asked me.

"What?" I couldn't tell what he was looking at.

"The *Cliffhanger*, Dad. The *big* slide."

"Hmm." I looked up at the biggest slide in the park. It

was a little intimidating, for anyone, much less someone the size of Jacob. "Sound good to you, Mom?"

"I guess so." Samantha didn't sound too sure.

"Let's go, buddy. I'll go with you."

We waited through a moderately long line, but we finally got to the top, where we only had a few people in line ahead of us. Jacob had gone from talkative to quiet in the last few minutes, and I suspected that he was having some last-minute second thoughts about this decision.

I leaned over and kept my voice at a level that only he could hear and said, "You know, it's okay if you're a little scared. That's just normal for something like this. Heck, *I'm* a little scared."

"Yeah?"

"Yeah."

We watched as a teenage guy became the next chambered round and laid down at the top of the chute. They had him cross his arms over his chest and wait. When the Schlitterbahn employee got the signal from below, that the path was safely cleared, he reached out and gave the kid a push and over he went.

It looked crazy!

Jacob watched and gave an almost imperceptible nod; he was accepting the challenge.

Jacob went next. My heart was in my throat when he was pushed over the edge. The guy let me watch until Jake was done with the vertical before I laid back and got ready myself. Moments later, he gave *me* that little push.

Over the edge I dropped. "Ah-oooh!" I went vertical and it felt like my back left the slide a little bit as gravity hurtled me toward the bottom of the slide. I was horizontal again soon. The combination of my fantastic speed and the shallow, pooled water at the bottom of the slide created a unique effect known to school kids globally as a *super-wedgie*.

As I tried to gracefully remove my shorts from my lower intestines, Jacob ran up to meet me, hollering, "That was *awesome*, Dad! It was *so* fast. How fast do you think we went?"

"Whew, man, I don't know…" Samantha was behind Jake, smiling over the top of his head at me. "Two or three hundred miles per hour?"

"Ha ha! I don't know either, but it was really, really fast."

"No joke. But that's how we do this!" We high-fived.

I put my arm around Jacob and hugged him close to me and he let me…for a minute. But that minute was the best. Then he bolted away from me to go tell Mike Jr. and Miranda about his death-defying ride.

Samantha slid up to me and took Jake's place next to me. I hugged *her* close this time. She didn't run away.

"That looked scary."

"It *was* scary. Jake thought twice about going when we were up there…but then he manned up and pushed through it." It may seem silly, but I was proud of him. Overcoming fears later in life can be very difficult if you don't have any practice. Jake wasn't going to have that problem.

Lately I had been thinking a lot about my life: evaluating and analyzing all the little bits and pieces. *Maybe I'm going through a mid-life crisis of some sort*, I wondered. I didn't think so, but you never know.

Samantha and I walked in peaceful silence and I watched her out of the corner of my eye.

I owed Samantha for stabilizing my life. She denies that she is the reason I'm not, best case, an alcoholic, or worst case, dead. She's made of good stuff—principles and traits that prevent her from taking credit for something like that. There is no denying, however, that I was in a bad, bad place when I met her and I didn't even realize it. She filled a void in my life. She also replaced those bad habits.

Of course, those bad habits all stemmed from high school and the notoriously unpredictable and strange world that surrounded me then…

Chapter 8
1991

"Is Billy going to hook us up?" Scott asked.

It was Friday night in the locker room, right after a game, and everybody was going a little crazy. We had beaten South Houston, our longtime rival, in a game that I thought I would remember my entire life. We were two teams at our best, playing our hardest, and nobody gave an inch.

Now everyone was loud, raucous, and ready to go out. We were three dozen teenage boys, jammed up with adrenaline, ready to meet girls, cause trouble, and drink beer. Never, in the history of the world, had there been a more perfect Texas night.

"Billy will indeed hook us up," I replied to Scott. "Need you even ask?"

"Well, you know, I just wanted to make sure."

"That's what I like about you, Scott. You are always looking out for our best interests," I told him. "Actually, Billy has everything in place already."

"He's a good man," Scott declared.

My dad had been feeding us beer since I could remember. He never went out of his way to give it to us, but he never put up a fight. In the beginning, it was just a natural response to kids' inquisitive "Dad, can I try some" requests.

A 7-year-old Jack might grab the can next to his dad and ask, "Can I have a drink?"

Naturally, Billy would agree. "Let 'er rip, Son." Jack's a man-in-training and you can never start training too early.

The first few years of this generally led to that young Jack spitting the beer out with a *Yuck!* After all, it was cheap stuff, and it didn't really taste good. The situation was a product of curiosity, not thirst, or need, and it only happened here and there. Those present whenever that happened, Billy's buddies through the years, would chuckle and slap their legs. Heck, most of them had gone through something similar as kids or did it with their own children. It's coming of age in Texas, ladies and gentlemen.

Add three years and the situation changes. Now young Jack is ten years old. Years of taste-testing, and the evolution, or toughening, of the boy's innards have made it easier to stomach that bitter, amber nectar worshipped by so many. Also changed is his awareness of those around him. No more spitting beer out in disgust. A slight scowl, perhaps, but that's it. In Texas, no *real* man spits out beer, even a teenager. It would be a travesty—an affront to all—and could result in immediate expulsion from any social group...or at least a reduction in standing.

If you jump forward yet another three or four years, we see Jack as a teenager. This is really when things get tricky. It's the nexus of home, school, and peers; a Bermuda Triangle of young adult life commonly referred to as high school. Only the most reserved or resolute of kids remain unaffected during these trying times when peer pressure, acceptance, and hormones dominate (confuse) the mind and body.

Yes, life was strange indeed for me, Jack Leonard, man-in-training.

So, my dad had begun making a keg available to the guys after games on the weekend. This propelled him to a legendary status amongst my friends. Billy never let things get crazy, but our house became a place where boundaries could be breached peaceably.

"Scott?"

"Yeah?"

"Do you have that CD I let you borrow?" I asked him.

"See dees nuts?" he returned. I stopped cold in the middle of putting on the polo I was wearing out that night. I gave him a blank stare, keeping my face as emotionless as possible.

"Umm, no." I kept staring at him and shook my head. "That was pretty weak. That joke is one dead horse that has been beaten and beaten and beaten."

He looked at me thoughtfully for a moment as he hiked up an arm and put on deodorant. "Yeah. Yeah, that was weak," he agreed. We both laughed at that.

We continued dressing a moment without speaking. I was vaguely aware of the conversations going on around us in the locker room.

Man, that interception was epic.

Dude, do you think that Jennifer is going to be there?

I think I'm getting ripped tonight!

It really didn't change much, what the guys all talked about. Leading topics were always the same: game, girls, and beer.

I finished tying up my shoes and closed my locker. "I was talking about the U2 album...*Achtung Baby!* Do you have it with you? I've really been pining for it. Yearning for it."

"I have it, bro. It's in my truck."

"Great."

The locker room was butted up against the players' and coaches' parking lot. Scott and I were the first two players to reach the double doors, which squealed with protest when we pushed through them, and made our way outside.

No matter how warm and humid a Texas night, it was cool on the skin and refreshing to the lungs after being in a Texas high school locker room. I stopped at the curb, dropped my duffel bag, and put my hands on my hips. The doors screeched and closed behind us.

"What a glorious, perfect night." I said. Scott stopped beside me, dropped his duffel bag, and looked up into the starry sky.

"Yeah," he agreed. We stood there for a few seconds. I can't speak for Scott, but I was enjoying the silence and relative calm that had enveloped me that moment.

Then the doors banged open behind us and someone howled, "Ahhhh-oooohhhh! Yeah!"

Without looking Scott said, "Nice blocks, John."

Big John lumbered up beside us. Scott's 6'4" frame was

dwarfed in comparison to John who was now a few inches taller and many pounds heavier than Scott. He already played a college-level game and we all figured that he would go pro.

"Yeah, baby. Ahhhh-oooooh!" he howled again, strolling across the parking lot to his truck. It roared to life, glasspacks firing off loudly—the sound of Texas.

I looked at Scott. He looked at me.

"Well...let's get tanked!"

~~~~~

It was a little after eleven o'clock when folks started arriving at my house. They came mostly in clumps of four to six: the number of teenagers that could be squeezed into a Honda Accord-sized sedan. First you heard the laughter, then the gate would swing open, and then you saw the people.

I was sitting next to the pool with a beer in my hand. Scott was next to me; he also had a beer in his hand. As guys came into view I exchanged *the nod* with most of them.

The nod was something I learned when I was, maybe, twelve years old, and it had carried on through high school. Nobody ever spoke of it. It was handed down non-verbally, a cultural gift. One day you noticed your friends were doing it, or their older brother was doing it, so you did it, too. Like a virus, it jumped from person to person, like that.

The nod had multiple meanings, but they all roughly translated into the same thing: *what's up?* but with a little extra confidence. The brainier kids in school didn't do it. At least not to us—they may have done it with each other.

Here's how the what's-up-nod worked.

First, a single, quick chin lift and head lift combo, in a controlled manner. Next, the slightest pause when your head reaches peak-lift position. Last, bring the chin and head back down. Done. A single up-and-down, just like that. The nod. Sometimes a slight chin thrust was appropriate. Sometimes a verbal exchange accompanied the nod. But, the nod was sufficient all on its own—it didn't need anything else.

My closer friends got a more animated response consisting of man-hugs, punches, jokes, and name-calling. This was not a book club gathering; we were football players. We weren't all dumb—I'm not saying that. But, there was a standard of behavior that called for a mixture of manliness and silliness.

If you look past the fact that my dad bought us all our booze, it was just like any high school party. In his defense, he enforced a zero tolerance policy on fights and overt hanky-panky. If things went in those directions, and he caught wind of it, he would show up and things would get relaxed *very* fast to avoid trouble. For the most part, everyone followed these basic rules so that we didn't lose any privileges.

Rarely was my dad to be found without beer nearby. My high school parties in his backyard were no different. He didn't hang out with us the entire night; however, he did come out to praise us on game nights after a win, or to commiserate with us on the nights we had losses. Thankfully, of course, we had a lot more of the former.

Billy would shake hands with the guys and give a nod to the girls. My mother occasionally accused him of ogling the girls, but if he did, I never noticed. He seemed much more interested in football and beer.

He'd talk to players and nonchalantly throw out his advice to the guys. He wasn't completely an armchair quarterback—he was a good player in his own heyday—but he was no Vince Lombardi either. He was just a guy that used to play football and still watched it voraciously.

Nonetheless, he routinely shocked the guys with some bizarre insight that made a positive change in their game. Sometimes this habit of backyard drunk-coaching my teammates annoyed me; sometimes it made me chuckle; but, most of the time I was oddly impressed with his ability to make sense out of the game even though he had surely taken down, in volume of alcohol, enough to bring down an elephant.

Then Billy would disappear for a while and let us be on our own.

"Billy's on a roll tonight," Scott said with no small measure of admiration in his tone. His own mother and father had divorced when he was young and his old man lived on the West Coast. If you were ever an audience to Scott's mom on the topic of Scott's father, you would get a not-so-subtle earful regarding his level of worthlessness. I think that, subconsciously, Scott thought of Billy as his father more than he did his actual father.

"Billy's drunk, brother," I told him.

"Man, Billy doesn't really get drunk," Scott argued. "Billy drives his Dodge truck to the intersection of beer and happy, finds a spot to park, and stays there all night and day. That's where he lives, man. That's where he lives."

I laughed. "You're right. He does stay in some weird place that is on the verge of drunkenness without ever getting there."

As we chuckled at our Billy jokes, a tall fellow named James came strolling around the side of the house with several girls in tow. He was about 6'7" so, naturally, we called him Little Jimmy. You could see that he was walking slowly so that the girls didn't have to sprint to keep up with his enormous stride. All in all, he was a very mellow guy who laughed at most everything. It made him easy to like.

Of course, Little Jimmy didn't play football—he played basketball. This meant he regularly suffered some grief from us—us being the football team.

"Ladies," Scott said, smirking, when Jim and his entourage of girls got to our chairs. I could tell that he was mostly just calling *Jim* a lady. Seeing the twinkle in Jim's eyes, I knew he got it.

"Scott. Jack." He nodded his head at us, but this time it wasn't the what's-up-nod. This was the more polite, speaking-with-an-equal nod, which was slower and consisted of one, curt downward nod from normal head position. No chin lift in this one.

"Jim, please introduce us to your lovely friends," Scott said.

"My pleasure...what we have here are four young ladies who are a *long* way from home, traveling deep into unknown territory...South Houston girls, just looking to have some fun."

"Well, ladies, let me tell you...you've come to the right

place..." Scott moved his hand between us with a grand, sweeping gesture and continued, "...we are connoisseurs of fun. I'm Scott..." It was hard not to chuckle at my buddy's bigger-than-life way of expressing himself. And he did it without arrogance, which made it magnetic to the people around him. I could already see that a couple of our newcomers' eyes were softening up and locking on to Scott. The girls laughed. "...that's Jack," he finished, pointing at me in highly dramatic fashion.

"South Houston, huh?" I asked them.

"Yeah. We thought it might be fun to meet some new people." That was girl #1—she wasn't one of the girls that had targeted Scott. I smiled at her.

"That should be easy enough. And...we won't tell anyone you were here," I told her with a wink. The girls laughed.

"Is this your house?" girl #2 asked. I noted that she darted her eyes toward Scott a couple of times while she asked me. *Not interested and I'm not surprised.*

"It is."

"Are your parents out of town or something?" she asked.

"No, not exactly, but there's no need to fret...everything is fine," I replied. Sometimes it was easier to avoid this topic than to explain to everyone that my dad allowed teenagers to get plastered at his house. Honesty frequently invited, at a minimum, strange looks, and the occasional additional questioning, which got old—fast. Sometimes it's just easier to roll with a situation instead of making things awkward and strange.

"Cool," Girl #1 said. She reached up and pushed her hair behind her ear. A simple gesture, but attractive. I smiled again to let her know I was interested.

"Refreshments are in the pool house," I told them (her). "It will flow freely all night without pause. The young ladies' room is also in the pool house, in the back," I said with a slightly overbearing flourish, but I could see the impact wasn't quite the same as when Scott did it. *Scott the Charmer*, I thought to myself. I noticed that girls #2 and #3 continued checking out Scott, trying to be subtle, but mostly failing. I wondered how much conflict there would be between *those* two tonight. Girls, I had found, could be surprisingly vicious about dudes, especially when *hitting the sauce.*

There was a fourth girl, but it looked like she was happy with Little Jimmy.

"Hey...thanks. I'm Jill, by the way."

"Ha, Jack and Jill!" Jimmy said, guffawing, looking at each of us in turn. A few of the girls cracked a smile, but the response was underwhelming. Jimmy looked around at us and asked, "You guys get it, right? Jack and Jill?" He laughed even harder, his lanky frame convulsing and shuddering with each gale.

Pretty soon we were all laughing. Spontaneous combustion, I guess.

The night continued in standard fashion after that. With our win, morale was high, and people were generally jubilant. Laughter could be heard around every corner. Like clockwork, a couple of guys got tossed in the pool. They took it in stride and took advantage of the opportunity to go shirtless around the girls. It was just another warm Texas night.

I played the good host and mingled with everyone. There was no one I didn't like. I knew that some of the team didn't take kindly to the non-athlete types in our school, and I didn't hate them for that, but it wasn't my personal policy. I enjoyed people. And, thanks to Dad's money, there was an amazing stereo system wired and playing music (at a moderate volume) outside and in every room. What could be better than people *and* music *and* beer?

I found myself, at one point, in the middle of a discussion on the merits of Victor Hugo's *Les Misérables*. Half of my honors-level English class was piled around the sofa in the pool house. This was in stark contrast to the parallel conversations happening outside.

The tamer kids, the brains, the middle-of-the-roaders, and the preps, usually gravitated to the pool house while the rowdier kids stayed outside. At least that's how the night usually started. Well, with the notable exception of the guys and girls who were feeling amorous. They could be found inside or outside.

The smartest kids, my English classmates, were drinking, too, but they were definitely a calmer group. They didn't always talk books or *smart* stuff though it was very nearly always less guttural than what my football bros were discussing. I was the lone ball player in most of their classes, which made me a novelty of sorts—the football player who liked books and things not sports—an endangered species.

"What did you think of *Les Misérables*, Jack?" one of them asked me.

"I enjoyed it. All the classic conflicts were involved...war, love, money and greed..." I stopped for just a second when I noticed that Jill was talking to someone nearby. She smiled at me. I gave a quick nod and smile in return. "And I really enjoyed it when we went to see the play."

"That was great," one girl said.

"Yeah, I loved the way the stage rotated in place so that they could portray travel and movement on the stage," said another.

"Me, too...that was my first time seeing anything like that." My family wasn't exactly the type that attended plays. We were, after all, rednecks at the core.

"Mrs. Bates is a great teacher. I'm so happy she took us to see it." Leslie was one of my favorites in the class, a dreamer, who saw the world through romantic eyes. She looked wistful.

"Leslie, you are a gem."

"Thanks, Jack." Her green eyes were bright, even in the dimly lit room, her face perpetually lit by her own positive life view. "Oh, *hey*, I like this song!" Leslie started bouncing her head to the music.

You burden me with your questions, you'd have me tell no lies...

I listened as EMF's *Unbelievable* came through the speakers and couldn't stop my own head from bobbing a little bit. Leslie and another English class girl, Marie, stood up and started dancing around to the music. It was one of those rare nights when everyone seemed to have harmonized and spirits were universally high. I didn't understand it; but, I didn't question it.

I made eye contact with Jill on my way out of the pool house; she smiled at me again. I returned the smile. We hadn't spoken much during the night, but that was okay—we routinely stayed in each other's periphery, dancing in and out of view, smiling, and having fun, playing boy-girl games.

It was close to 3am when things began to wind down. Over half the guests had departed in the last hour and I was feeling a little tired and a little drunk. Some people would stay all night, sleeping in various positions and places around the pool house. On rare occasions, someone crashed on a lounge chair on the back patio. At the end of the night, if I hadn't passed out, I would walk around and toss some towels and blankets on people.

I should mention that, perhaps, the stoutest rule of all for these little soirees was that nobody entered the main house. That edict was handed down from Mom. A few close friends of mine were allowed to break this rule, just to use a quiet restroom, but nobody else. My mother, while she reluctantly allowed all of this, did not want people destroying her house. She considered the pool house to be my father's domain—an acceptable loss. And, it was big enough to satisfy the *needs* of teenagers.

I made another round through the thinning groups and found our entire offensive line dipping and spitting at one of the tables near the pool. "What's up, fellas?"

"Jack. Nothin', man. Dip?" Jones asked and laughed. The last time we were all out together was down in Galveston, where one of the player's older brother rented us a hotel room. It was right on the seawall and there were people everywhere. One of these guys offered me chewing tobacco. It was my first time trying it—and my last. I was halfway through a bottle of Jack Daniel's when I took a huge chunk of the brown stuff *at the goading of these same guys* and put it in my mouth. It tasted weird, at first, but not bad.

I didn't know what I was doing, I was drunk, and I swallowed the whole lot of it. I rushed to the balcony with a hand clamped on my mouth and threw up over the side. All the night's alcohol poured out of me, along with the dip, and a Big Mac. It was pretty much an awful experience and it was only a miracle that no one was down below.

"Yeah, no thanks, Jonesy, but I appreciate you thinkin' of me."

"Dude, that was some seriously funny shit, man, you puking off that balcony. I will never forget that. Texas Jack! Ha ha!"

"I wonder what the employees thought of *that* little mess they had to clean up." That was Jason Kelso. He was a mostly quiet guy, but when he did talk, it was usually surprisingly sarcastic or funny.

"Yeah...it looked just like Texas. You totally threw up the state of Texas," another guy said.

"That was the best part. You just can't make up something like that."

"Jason...didn't you take a picture of it?"

"Oh, man, I did! I'm gonna have to get that film developed."

They talked about my vomit for another 10 minutes. I'll confess—it was funny—but it doesn't change the fact that I never wanted to try dip again.

"You guys know you can crash here, right?"

"We're good. Jones didn't drink. He's takin' us all home."

We did a variety of man-hugs, and handshake-like

actions, which all meant *good-bye* though nobody in this group would ever say the words *good-bye*. It was always *peace* or *laters* or *I'm out* and the secret handshakes and butt slaps.

I continued my rounds. I noticed Jill was still present and accounted for, which intrigued me. We acknowledged each other and I could see that there was still plenty of tension and connection between us. She was with a small group on the other side of the yard. *That's my next stop.*

Scott had, at some point, settled into deeper discussion and minor petting with girl #2. *So, that's how that played out*, I thought to myself.

My *seal* was broken and now multiple restroom breaks were inevitable as long as I remained awake. If I had a nickel for every time I heard someone say, "I broke the seal," I'd have at least a few dollars. I opened a door that led into what my mother called our mudroom so that I could make a quick pit stop.

An odor assaulted my nostrils almost as soon as I was inside. *Cigarettes.* My dad had a small study in this corner of the house and would occasionally sneak a cigarette when he thought Mom wasn't paying attention. He even had this little *As Seen On TV* gadget that claimed to pull the smoke out of the air. I wouldn't know about it if he hadn't left it running one night. It didn't work.

I shook my head a little. The smell was pungent and there was no way Mom was going to miss this one.

When I opened the study door smoke discharged into the hallway. It wasn't thick, but it was enough to indicate something was wrong. A quick survey showed me exactly what it was: my father had passed out holding a lit cigarette.

There weren't flames; the situation wasn't that dire. I grabbed the quilted Texas A&M throw that was on the other end of the sofa, a gift from my mom to my dad, and quickly patted down the smoldering area beside my snoring father.

"Dad!" I hissed quietly. No reaction.

"Ouch," I continued to dab at the cushion, burning my

finger tips. Looking around, I grabbed his cup, half full of beer, and poured it on the couch. There was some hissing and it seemed that the material was no longer burning.

"Holy shit, dude!" I turned to see Scott had come in behind me.

"Can you fill this up with water?" I handed him the red plastic cup, and with a heave, moved my dad to the other side of the couch. His snoring escalated, then changed pitch, but he didn't wake up. Scott came back in with the cup, and without question, doused the throw and the couch.

"It's out, bro," Scott exclaimed. "Wow."

"Yeah...wow." I was disturbed and a little angry. I muttered some curse words, thinking about it. My dad was just lying there—he had barely moved, much less awakened, and he could have burned the place down!

"What are you going to do?" Scott was quiet. Events had sobered him up and he had a very somber look on his face.

"I guess I'm going to try and clean this up and air out the room. I don't think I can hide this from my mom either. Look at the *hole* he put in the couch..." I waved my hand in the general direction of my father's victim: our sofa. My head was starting to hurt. I needed to get some aspirin soon or I was going to go crazy from the dull thrum in my head.

"*Jack?*" I jerked my head when I heard the female voice down the hallway. Any other day the sound would have been pleasant, but it was horrible timing, and I wasn't interested anymore. Not tonight.

I moved out into the hallway and came face to face with Jill. She smiled brightly and asked me, "Is everything okay? I thought you were going to come talk to me some more." She moved closer, just inches from me, and the glassy eyes that stared up at me told me the whole story: she was a little beyond tipsy. She crinkled her nose distractedly and said, "Are you cooking? It smells like something is burning." She was still looking at me though, unperturbed by the indication of fire. Minutes ago I would have really been into her and moving with the flow, but the momentum was gone. The magic hat was empty—no rabbit.

"Hey, I was going to come find you soon...I really wanted to talk to you more, " I told her. "But, I had something come up and now I have some things to take care of..."

It took a second for Jill to grasp this information. I waited, watching her for telltale signs of eruption. I had seen many people drunk, girls and guys, and you never knew if a drunk was going to have their fuse get ignited over something silly and ridiculous.

Jill didn't look happy about it, but she accepted the news once I agreed to take her phone number. "You can call me tonight, if you want," she told me, blinking her eyes slowly at me and leaning into me again. I didn't want to be rude, but I was drained of energy.

"Okay, Jill. I'll try. But I have to go right now. Can Scott walk you out?"

"Okay," she breathed and gave me a quick kiss. It was nice, but again, bad timing.

Scott moved toward the door and Jill managed to keep her balance as she walked backwards a few steps, giving me the look. I almost felt bad about it. I had no intention of calling her.

I let out a long sigh. Life was a strange beast, full of surprises. While opportunities had risen, they were quickly smothered by *burning* responsibilities. I turned back to the business of cleaning up my dad and restoring as much order as possible to my little world.

Chapter 9
Wednesday, August 8th, 2012

"Whaddaya have going on there, Jake? What are you playin'?" Billy set his beer down on the end table and sat down in the recliner to watch his grandson. Jake's hands and fingers deftly flickered around on the video game controller in his hands.

"Grandpa, come on, you bought the games! It's MLB 2012…the baseball game," Jake said excitedly, engrossed in the game. Billy heard the roar of the crowd and shifted his focus from Jake to the high definition television screen. Indeed, larger than life, there were giant, cartoonish baseball players all over the screen—cartoonish, yet, realistic too. Billy chuckled to himself when he heard the *announcers* in the game comment on the bases being loaded.

"Can I play, too?" he asked Jake.

"Yeah Grandpa," Jake replied. "Just let me exit out of this game. You can pick your own players and make your own team. It's really cool. Do you want me to do it for you? I can just ask you about players and you tell me yes or no or whatever." Jake hit some more buttons and the game he was playing stopped. Menus were soon on the television screen.

"That sounds good, buddy. Can I be the Rangers?" Billy watched, amused, as Jake began thumbing through menus and players. His little fingers moved rapidly.

"Grandpa, *you* can't be the Rangers. *I'm* the Rangers!"

"Oh, man, Jake…I don't know if I can be any other team."

"Grandpa!" Jake exclaimed.

"Jake!"

"Grandpa!" he said again.

"Oh, okay…I guess I can be someone else. Make me the Astros. It just won't be the same though…and it's gonna hurt watching the Astros beat the Rangers. I'm not sure God will be happy with us, Jake."

Jake laughed. "I don't think you have anything to worry about, Grandpa. The Rangers *are* going to win." They both laughed.

"Can you go ahead and pick my players for me? I'm going to hit the restroom."

"Okay, Grandpa. I'll make you a good team. *Almost* the best."

Billy laughed, drained the rest of his beer, and got up from the recliner. At the doorway he stopped a beat, looked back, and admired Jake. His grandson, the only one who could carry on the family name. Billy couldn't imagine there being a better grandson. He could tell already that Jake was going to be a good person. *Probably won't make all those mistakes I made,* he figured. *He's already got a better head on his shoulders than me. Like his daddy.*

After he was done in the restroom, Billy stepped into the kitchen and opened the refrigerator. He saw that he had six bottles of beer remaining and he'd already had a few. *How many?* he wondered, but he couldn't remember. *Maybe five already. Six? Hmm. I still have the keg downstairs...Nah, I shouldn't need that. I won't drink that much.*

"William, you did remember that I am volunteering today? Didn't you?"

Billy jumped. "Lainey! Snuck right up on me...tryin' to give me a heart attack?"

"That's funny...I didn't think that drunks got scared."

"I am *not* drunk."

"Hmm." She regarded him closely. "No, I don't guess you're drunk. Yet. You're not going to get drunk though, are you? You'll have to watch Jake alone tonight. Jack and Samantha are going out."

"Lainey. He's eleven years old. He can practically take care of himself..."

"No, he's *ten* years old for a few more days, and he's not

self-sufficient." She lowered her voice, adding, "He's still a little boy and believe it or not, little boys need supervision." The tone of her voice was gentle, but firm, and after almost forty years together, Billy had learned when to go ahead and give up. His own father had called him mule-headed, an apt description if ever there was one. He didn't always stick to the letter of the law of what was being said, but he figured it was too tiring to argue about stuff. And it was easier to ask for forgiveness later. *Especially* when he had the pleasure of his grandson being there. *Heck, she's probably right anyway*, he thought. *This time, ha!*

He tucked his head down just a bit, lifted one eyebrow, and replied, "Okay dear."

~~~~~

Samantha and I were excited about having a day out together. Work, school, and Jacob's swimming had kept us busy that year. On those rare occasions that we had some free time, we made a family day of it, instead of taking some time to be alone. We agreed that family time was the priority, and that our needs as a couple, and as individuals, were lower on the totem pole.

Of course, two people need to invest time and stay connected. That, or risk losing touch. We were excited about a day out together without responsibilities. A day of frolic and fun.

"It's great being back in Galveston. I know we were just here, but I love it, and we didn't go to the beach Sunday anyway," Samantha said. We were just crossing the apex of the Causeway. I tapped the button to lower the windows, so that I could smell the salt in the air. I gulped it down; I couldn't get enough.

"Yeah...I love it, too," I agreed. "Sometimes I wonder if we should have moved here instead of Austin." The wind was whipping around in the car. We didn't ride with the windows down much—Samantha didn't like the uncontrollable way it moved her hair around—but she never complained when we went to Galveston.

"Hmm. That's always something to think about. Of course, there are the hurricanes."

"True." My uncle Paul, my mother's brother, had lived in Galveston almost his entire adult life. His home was small, but it was barely a 10-minute walk from the beach. Mom, Katie, and I would go down to see Uncle Paul and Aunt Tracey, and they'd take us across the street for picnics in the sand. As a kid, I always looked forward to those quick trips to Galveston.

Tragedy hit the first time in 1990. A drunk driver stole

Aunt Tracey from Paul. He weathered the storm, but was never the same, and we saw him only infrequently after that. Paul turned to a quiet life in the church and found his solace there.

Tragedy struck again in 2008. That time, it was Hurricane Ike, a daring, but capable thief and destroyer of dreams. Ike filled Paul's house with water that didn't retreat for days. Ike also set a tree down on Paul's roof. The damage was great and insurance declared it a total loss. There was water damage from floor to ceiling in almost every room. By the time two men in biohazard-type suits removed Uncle Paul's refrigerator, it had been sitting through 90-degree-Fahrenheit days for weeks. Thankfully, Paul had evacuated early, but after he swept up the broken remains of what had been his home and possessions, he moved away and put Galveston in the rear view mirror of his memory.

Still, through good or bad times, Galveston was enchanting and enduring. There was something magical about *the island* that kept us coming back.

Soon enough my reverie was broken and we were exiting and turning right onto 61st Street. A flood of memories hit me every time that I was on the island. We were moving serenely along the low bridge that straddled part of the Galveston Bay.

"When we used to come here in high school, we'd sometimes rent Jet Skis right there." I pointed at a parking area alongside the bridge. "I wonder where the guy went that ran that get-up. He just had this piece of plywood near his lean-to with 'Jet Ski Rental' painted on it in bright red. We paid like 25 bucks to rent one for an hour. It was great."

"Yeah..." Samantha said. I glanced her way. She was looking at the water as it passed by, but looked at me as if on cue, or like she had a sixth sense. Her eyes twinkled with humor.

"I probably mentioned that before."

"Maybe." She smiled. "Maybe every time we cross this bridge."

"Okay, alright, maybe so. Those were fun times. Young, dumb, and full of fun."

"You and Scott, terrorizing the poor local girls, I'm sure."

"Probably not the local girls so much—they stayed away from us. We were dangerous. Outsiders. Tough guys. You remember. I'm sure it's what attracted you to me."

Samantha laughed and I watched her out of the corner of my eye. Still so beautiful. Those soft brown, almond-shaped eyes, and the perfectly white smile—she was incredible. Whatever Cupid-like powers existed out there, bringing people together, they had favored me. Big time.

"Tough," I said again and flexed my bicep for emphasis.

A few minutes later we turned left onto Seawall Boulevard. Even though it was a Wednesday, the island was packed, and I could only imagine that there were tens of thousands of visitors today. Cars lined the beach. Bodies, darkened by the golden discus in the sky, walked lazily up and down the walkway. Bicyclists periodically darted in-and-out between the walkers. We crept along at 25 miles per hour—the fastest we could move—since the motorists were busy watching tanned skin, calling to people from open windows, and in general, being island tourists.

"Parking is probably going to be ugly," I murmured. While I was enjoying watching all the people, I couldn't help but notice...*there are a lot of people!*

"Well, they made a parking lot, right?"

"I guess so. It's across the street. We'll see. Maybe I'm just being cynical."

It took us another ten minutes, but we made it to the pier. I had to admit—it looked fantastic. It reminded me of the Santa Monica Pier in California except smaller.

"Wow! Looks like fun!" Samantha exclaimed. Her excitement was contagious. *She was contagious!*

"Yeah, it does. There's the parking lot. Let's see if we can get lucky." I made the turn, zipping across the street to avoid the oncoming traffic, and entered the lot. Miracle of miracles, we found a space coming open—a very large truck was leaving—and the Land Rover fit nicely in the void it left.

"Bubba Gump first, Jack. I'm starving."

"Sounds great, gorgeous. I'm always down for some shrimp." We shut down my baby and gathered our stuff. "I'll tell Jake that we had seafood when we get back to my parents' house. He'll be glad he didn't come tonight."

"Yep. That little picky guy. How can you not like seafood?"

"It's a mystery to me," I replied. I noticed that Samantha had our camera bag in her lap. "Are we going to haul around the good camera? I have my iPhone 4 Sssss…" I hissed.

"I guess not. I'll just put it behind my seat. Will you hold my ID card?"

"Yes, dear."

"And, my lipstick?"

"Yes, dear."

"You're good to me."

"Yes, dear." She laughed and leaned into me as we walked across the parking lot. I surreptitiously leaned in close to her hair and inhaled. I was several inches taller than Samantha which had afforded me this opportunity the entire time we had known each other. Her hair always smelled great; even sweaty it was alluring and natural. This never ceased to amaze me. When I was sweaty—it was unpleasant, to put it nicely. Not so with my wife. She somehow defied all the rules of nature in this regard.

~~~~~

"Oh, man, Grandpa! I just struck you out *again!*" Jake squealed. "That's going to be six in a row, Grandpa...two innings...the *first* two innings."

"Well, I'm not sure I've got these buttons right. Did you show me the wrong buttons on purpose, or something? Were you tricking Grandpa?"

"*Grandpa...*"

"Well, show me what's what again. Help an old guy out."

"Okay. Let me pause it." Jake hustled over to where his grandfather was tilted back in his large, leather recliner, and began his third tutorial on what the different buttons did. "For batting, use this one, but you have to time it ahead of the pitch. Okay?"

"Okay, buddy. I think I got it now. You can play it again whenever you're ready. I'll make sure I hit a grand slam." Billy reached over for a quick pull from his bottle of beer, which was, mysteriously, now empty.

"Oops. Wait just a minute, Jake. I'll be right back." Like a doctor making his rounds, Billy made his way to the restroom for a liquid delivery, then over to the kitchen. Inside the stainless steel refrigerator things were grim. *Only two beers left,* he noted, with some consternation to himself. *Well, I may have to tap into that keg after all.*

"Grandpa..." Jake hollered. "Come on—it's ready!"

"Coming, little dude!" Billy hollered back. He popped open his bottle and tossed the cap in the trashcan in a fluid movement that came from decades of practice. He ambled into the living room, feeling mellow. Perched on the edge of the couch now, Jake looked ready for action, and Billy couldn't suppress a smile. "Okay, Jake. Gramps is back. Time to show you what an old-timer can do."

"Ha ha, okay. Ready?"
"Ready."

~~~~~

"Hi, my name is John, I'll be your server today. Do you guys need some more time to look at the menu, maybe start with drinks?" Our Bubba Gump waiter was chipper and his delivery was well-oiled and slick.

"We're ready to order," Samantha said. I was always impressed by her ability to make ultra-quick decisions when it came to menu selections. "Right, Jack?"

"Absolutely, babe." On the other hand, I always needed more time to look at the menu, but I always denied the fact that I needed more time. I always told Samantha that I was ready when she asked. Her rhythm was just so perfect—seemed to me it would be a crime to disturb it.

"Okay. I'll have the Shrimper's Net Catch, two-thirds pound, and a Coke."

"Excellent, Ma'am, and you, Sir?" The waiter turned to me inquiringly.

"Very good, then. I'll have a Bloody Mary, a steak sandwich, and a steak sandwich."

"Sir?" The waiter looked confused.

"Just a joke," I laughed. I cast a quick glance over the menu again. A few seconds passed before my eyes landed on something interesting. "Baja shrimp tacos, my man," I told him, slapping my menu closed.

"To drink, Sir?"

Ah! Another choice to make—so quickly on the heels of the last. "Hmm…I'll have a Coke, too."

"Excellent. I'll put your orders in and drinks will be here shortly." John removed our menus and was gone in a flash. He was robotic, yet fast, and not without personality…but it was like a rehearsed personality. I wondered briefly if I had imagined him being there—that's how fast it seemed to happen.

"Okay. What was that?" Samantha asked. "Let me guess…something from a movie, right?"

"You know me so well. It's from Fletch…Chevy Chase…when they're at the tennis club?"

"Nope. Don't remember," she said.

"No, of course not. How about our waiter…he's a slick one, isn't he?"

Samantha laughed. "He is definitely practiced in his motions. He has achieved equilibrium between his work needs and his persona. Economy of motion. Economy of action."

"Huh," I grunted, pausing, thinking about it. "Where did you get that?"

"I made it up."

I laughed and she laughed, too. Then, I leaned in close and looked her in the eyes, those brown almonds, and told her, "I love you."

"I love you, too," she replied.

It was a pleasant moment, and I started to do the *I'm-leaning-in-to-kiss-you* move, when John crashed the scene with our drinks, robotically chipper, saying: "Two Cokes and your food should be out fast…the kitchen is doing great today!"

"Thanks, John," Samantha told him.

John left our table quickly and I was glad, because I could barely contain the laughter that bubbled up inside of me. As soon as he was out of earshot, I started laughing. "Yeah, thanks a lot, John."

~~~~~

"Here it comes, here it comes..." Jake was standing up near the television, urgently pressing the buttons on his controller. "That's strike two!"

The video game commentators were getting excited and the living room was filled with the buzz and sounds of baseball. Billy leaned forward in his chair. He was actually getting the hang of things (sort of) and having a good time. Then again, he always had a good time when Jake was around.

"This might be the last pitch, Grandpa..." Jake taunted Billy.

"Don't count your chickens, buddy. It's not over *yet!*" The *players* in the living room were tense as the players on the television got into position. The pitcher went into the windup and Jake's fingers were flying. Billy watched as the ball was released. Everything seemed to slow down. He waited. He felt like he was in the zone on this one. He swung the bat.

Thump!

"Steeeerike three!" Jake pumped his hand in a victory *yes!*

"Oh, man! You got me, buddy!"

"Awesome game, Grandpa!"

"Yep. That was a good game—a lot of fun. At least the Rangers won," Billy said, chuckling. His heart rate was up, and he marveled that he almost felt like he had been playing in an actual game. "Pretty realistic how they make these games."

"Yeah, it's really cool. Thanks for getting it."

"No problem, buddy. Do you want to try that racing game? Do something else?"

"Can we go swimming? I've been practicing a lot for this next year and I'm pretty fast now."

"Sure, dude. Go get your trunks on and I'll meet you by the pool."

"Are you gonna swim, too?"

"Absolutely...for a little bit anyway. I'm old, ya know?"

"Ha. Right, Grandpa. Meet you outside!" Jake exclaimed and bolted from the room. Billy chuckled to himself as he stood, swaying a little bit, in the suddenly silent living room. *Oh, man, to have the energy that kids have,* he thought, bumping into just a single end table as he vectored himself to the kitchen.

Billy's gait had gradually changed as the hours passed. In the morning, swift and sure, by afternoon it had become slower, and in Billy's opinion, even more sure. His subconscious mind never accepted that his senses were compromised. His conscious mind didn't accept it either. In defiance of nature, he thought of himself as *more* capable and *more* lucid.

This defiance led to the legendary focus that only a certain kind of drunk can muster. Unnoticeable to himself, he was a mite slower in all of his actions: walking across the kitchen; opening the refrigerator door; and registering the fact that he was out of bottled beer. It all took longer as his mind overcompensated for the chemical changes taking place in his body.

Of course, he and the stainless steel refrigerator were great companions—made for each other. One held beer and kept it cold; the other drank cold beer.

He couldn't be angry. Besides, he was prepared for this contingency.

Billy went to his bedroom and changed into some swimming trunks. He stopped briefly to look at his reflection in the dresser mirror. *Not too bad for a guy in his late fifties,* he thought. His midsection was a little more *swollen* than it used to be, but otherwise, he thought things looked pretty good. He sucked in his stomach a little bit for a few seconds and checked the mirror again. He was getting softer though—it was hard to deny. The middle was extending beyond the chest. *Ah, well...nobody's perfect,* he mused, allowing his stomach to explode outward when he exhaled.

A young Seth Leonard witnessed Billy's tomfoolery from one end of the dresser. Seth—a good man—but a heavy drinker from a long line of heavy drinkers. Billy picked up the frame with his dad's black & white picture and his thoughts flitted briefly to his house, this house, and how, in the end, his father had given him that. Of course, his father had also given him beer.

Billy put the photograph back, and in accordance with Lainey's many requests, used the mudroom door to get to the backyard. Elaine was somewhat methodical about the house and she claimed that this kept it cleaner. He didn't really get the need for such caution since they had a lady that cleaned twice each week, but he acquiesced.

As soon as one of Billy's feet hit the cool tile of the back patio, Jake jumped up from where he was sitting on the diving board. "Can I jump in, Grandpa?"

"Okay, Michael Phelps—go for it."

The words were scarcely out of Billy's mouth and Jake was airborne from the end of the diving board and splashing into the deep end of the pool. A few seconds later he shot up the ladder and was out of the pool, trotting for the diving board again. "Watch this, Grandpa!" he hollered. He sprang forward, bounced off the end of the diving board, and performed a very graceful...*cannonball!* Water splashed as far, wide, and high as a 10-year-old boy could have hoped. He popped up a few seconds later. "How was it?"

"Huge splash, buddy. Huge. You'd definitely take the gold medal for cannonballs. Awesome."

"Awesome," Jake agreed. He began randomly splashing and horsing around.

Billy smiled as his grandson played. He recognized that Jacob was on that delicate cusp between extreme youth and young adulthood. He thought Jake looked a lot like Jack at that age. And himself, too, he supposed. The genetics were obvious in their family. Jake talked to himself as he started some imaginary pool adventure and Billy chuckled softly.

Billy made his way over to the pool house, opened the door, and flipped on the light. He grabbed a plastic cup from the cupboard above the oven and went to his keg refrigerator. It was a beautiful, commercial grade model that held two full-size kegs of beer. Billy's first truck cost, maybe, half of what this beer-cooling contraption had. He tilted the tap forward, filled his cup with ice-cold beer, and went back outside. *That's more like it.*

As he walked within a few feet of the edge of the pool, water splashed across him, soaking his legs and most of his back. The temperature wasn't iceberg, but it was chilly enough to alter the old heartbeat a little bit. "Jake!" he bellowed good-naturedly.

"Betcha can't get me Grandpa!"

"Oooh, boy, you're in for it now!" Billy proclaimed. He hurriedly set his beer down next to his favorite lounger and made a dash at the pool. He had life experience on his side; however, that didn't equalize the situation. For one, Jake swam like a fish. Two, Billy was working on being two or three sheets to the wind. Jake evaded his grandpa but was wise enough at his young age to intentionally keep things close. This kept Grandpa interested and in the pool.

The chase progressed around the pool towards the diving board. Jake opted for a quick jump off the diving board even though he suspected that Grandpa would catch up to him upon reentry into the water. He was right.

"I got you, little man!" Billy cried out triumphantly, grabbing a wildly giggling Jacob after he came up for air. He hauled Jake to the middle of the pool where he could stand comfortably and assail his grandson with random tickling, squeezing, and easy-going noogies. He may not be as quick in the pool, but his grandson's laughter was music to his ears.

"I can't breathe Grandpa!" he gasped in between laughing and howling. Billy let up on him and the two caught their breath a little bit.

I wonder if Grandpa knows I let myself get caught, Jacob thought briefly. He was a thoughtful kid—he would never tell. He was also smart—he knew his grandpa was drunk. He could smell the beer on his breath when he exhaled. Also, his grandpa's eyes were red and his face looked a little funny. *Puffy.* They had already learned about drugs and alcohol in school. He knew it was bad for you if you had too much. He suspected his grandpa was guilty of having too much.

"You let me catch you, didn't you, Jake?" his grandpa asked him with a gleam in his eye.

"No, Grandpa...I would *never* do that," he answered.

"Oh, yeah? Well, how about...I give you a *body slam!*" Billy said as he lifted Jake, already giggling again, and splashed him down into the water like a body slam. The two then tussled, wrestled, and laughed, enjoying the perfect weather and their time together.

"Whew! Okay, Jake," Billy announced after they had been going at it for another 10 minutes. "This old guy is tired. Do you mind playing by yourself while I lay down and get some sun for a bit?" he asked his grandson.

"Sure, Grandpa."

"Okay, Michael Phelps. Don't get too crazy."

"I won't," Jake replied.

Billy slogged his way over to the concrete stairs in the shallow end—he didn't have the energy to climb the ladder in the deep end—and stepped out of the pool. He stretched and yawned as the sun beat down on his tanned torso. He was no stranger to the pool. Jake had pointed out on a previous visit that some of the hair on his chest was white. Since then he had noticed it frequently himself.

He ambled over to the lounger (and his beer) as Jake soared through the air from the diving board. He plopped down and sipped his cup of quasi-cool beer and watched his grandson. Every now and then, life was just perfect.

Jake continued jumping, splashing, and entertaining himself as any 10-year-old boy might do. He hardly noticed when his grandfather drifted off to sleep.

~~~~

"Oh, my goodness, that was so much fun!" Samantha's face was alive with color. I slid my arm around her waist as we stepped down from the Iron Shark Rollercoaster. The boardwalk was teeming with people and we walked along it slowly. I quickly found myself lost in thought.

My life isn't dominated by superstitious behaviors; however, I am not immune to them. For someone who has played a lot of sports, it's inevitable. You end up repeatedly doing those things you think bring you luck: kissing a medallion; listening to a particular song; or, a quick prayer before the big game.

By the same token, if you suspect in the slightest that something is bad luck, you get rid of it. Or you change it. Or you redirect it. Fast. The competitive nature of sports requires quick action.

Sometimes, it's your gut that is telling you something is right or wrong—an innate impulse or guidance system. *Instinct.* Your instincts can be like this confusing, gray area between superstition and the subconscious. I've seen people win and lose when they followed their instincts.

But, I trusted mine. And they were telling me something was *wrong*.

"Jack?" Samantha was looking up at me expectantly.

"Sorry...did I miss something? I was zoning out a little bit."

"I just asked if you wanted to ride the rollercoaster again," she replied.

"No..." I couldn't stop my brows from furrowing or a small frown from tugging the corners of my mouth downward. My insides started to ache a little bit.

"Are you okay?" I could see the concern in Samantha's eyes.

"I just have a strange feeling," I told her. I didn't want to raise an alarm just because *I had a feeling.* "Let's call my parents and check on Jake."

"Okay." The quizzical look on Samantha's face might have struck me as funny another time.

I pulled my cell phone from my pocket and hit dial on the contact labeled *Billy & Lainey.*

~~~~~

Billy's snoring could have been the reason the term *sawing logs* was coined. It was loud. How Elaine slept right next to him was a mystery to those with the misfortune of having heard it.

Jake was oblivious to the snoring. He was just about to finish an epic struggle in what he considered the most awesome of Olympic swimming events: the individual medley. Jake had watched the 200- and 400-meter races on television the week before and was really excited when Michael Phelps, who was sort of his hero, had won a medley and Ryan Lochte had won the other medley. All week, he had been imagining that he was the captain of Team USA.

Jake thought that all swimming events were great, but the medley was definitely the best. The medley tested the swimmer on four different strokes in just one race. *How can you top that?* Not the team medley, of course, since each person did only one stroke. *That's not really a challenge...it's what we do anyway,* Jake figured. The individual medley, now, that was something!

He was really good at the backstroke and front crawl, and his breaststroke was improving. What he spent the most time practicing was his butterfly stroke. That was where he stood to see the most improvement, but he was a fast learner, and practice had been paying off. He was only ten, sure, but he had been taking swimming lessons since he was only three years old. And this year he had been swimming so much after school with the local intramural swim team.

When the house phone rang the first time, Jake had just started his first stroke, and was splashing or underwater. It's debatable whether *Superman* would have heard the faint ringing of the phone, which was across the living room, behind closed doors. For a preoccupied boy—impossible.

Billy *might* have been able to hear the phone. His lounger was close to the house and he didn't have splashing water as interference. That is, of course, if Billy were not passed out.

The phone went unanswered.

~~~~~

It didn't take much for me to talk Samantha into going back to my parents' house. She may have thought I was overreacting, but if so, she said nothing. Besides, she was cursed with a hyper-responsive maternal affliction…caring a great deal for her son. Perhaps my own concern was the catalyst, but she was now equally eager to check on Jacob. In Samantha's world, checking up on Jake *was* never, *could* never, be a waste of time.

She pulled the cell phone away from her ear when *Billy and Lainey* connected, but went to voice mail again. "Still no answer, Jack."

I grimaced only slightly and focused on the traffic as we left the Causeway behind us. It was only a feeling, but the feeling had intensified, and my senses told me that something bad was happening. Sometimes my hunches didn't pan out, but sometimes…

Sometimes they did.

"I'm sorry, Sam. I just don't like this feeling I have in the pit of my stomach."

"I understand…let's just get back and check on them. Probably nothing, but better safe than sorry, right?"

"Right," I agreed.

We were still 20 minutes away.

~~~~~

Just as his mom and dad were leaving the bridge to Galveston, heading north on I-45, Jake jumped out of the pool. As predicted, he had led Team USA to another round of gold medals.   A crowd of thousands had applauded and demonstrated their appreciation for his phenomenal leadership of the swimming team.

Now though, he needed a new challenge, and he knew what that challenge would be. He looked around for the cup of change that he was sure he had left out the last time they visited Grandma and Grandpa. He walked over to the patio and scanned beneath the three green tables there, but didn't see it.

Then he remembered: *the bench!* There was a white, wooden lattice decorated bench along the brick wall that bordered the garage around the side of the house. Grandma had said that she would keep his things out there.

He ran over to the bench and lifted up the seat. There was his super soaker (*awesome*); a variety of athletic balls and equipment; and other odds and ends. At the bottom of the compartment was a cup full of coins. *Score!*

Jacob emptied the coins into his hand and counted them—twelve. He tossed the little, plastic cup back in, closed the bench, and raced back over to the pool. He thought about how best to play his game, then turned around with his back facing the water. With one swift movement, he tossed all twelve coins into the pool behind him. He waited a few seconds, sprinted to the diving board, and then jumped in to search for the money. He called it *coin diving.*

He had some rules that he had made up on previous coin diving expeditions to make it even harder. The first rule was that you didn't look at where you threw the coins. The second rule was that you didn't look into the water before you jumped in. The final rule was that you had to get more than one coin each time you went under the water. He followed all three rules strictly—he wasn't the kind of boy that cheated.

It took him four dives, but Jake was able to round up all of the coins. He swam over to the ladder, clutching the change in his fist, and climbed out of the deep end of the pool. Stepping to the edge, with his back to the water, he silently decided that this time he would do it in just three tries. Then he hurled the money backwards. He heard the small *plup!* As individual coins entered the water and hoped all of them made it into the pool—he had overthrown before—but he didn't hear anything hit the concrete.

He waited a few seconds like he always did. As he waited, a shadow passed over Jake, and he noticed the sky had increased in cloudiness quite a bit. He mentally registered the clouds and the sound of his grandfather snoring.

Then, turning without looking downward into the water, he dived in and started his search. He covered the shallow side of the pool first and retrieved five coins before he burst up through the surface and caught his breath. *Awesome,* he thought, *I'll do this in three dives easy.*

He took a deep breath and went down again. This time he made his way around the deep end. As he passed by the drain in the center of the pool, he thought he saw the glint of silver, but he quickly passed by since he was almost out of breath. This time he had four coins when he kicked off the bottom of the pool and came up near the ladder. He held on for a second, set the nine coins he had found on the lip of the pool, then ducked under for what he was confident would be his last dive.

Three more to go, he thought as he moved his arms and propelled himself to the bottom of the pool. He quickly found the first coin in the corner. The copper of the penny blended with the shadow and he almost missed it.

A moment later he spied the second coin—a quarter— maybe three feet from the drain. He snatched it up and then turned around, eyes open under the water, to find the very last coin. He was doing well on time; he still felt like he had plenty of air left. *I just need to find the last coin!*

Then he remembered that he saw something in the drain.

He swam over and looked down inside. It was difficult to see anything or even tell how large the space was below. Where was the silver gleam he saw before? The clouds had taken away the power of the sun's assistance and it was harder to see.

Then he thought he saw it again, but it was so hard to tell. He didn't think that the holes in the grate were big enough to let a coin get in there, but he didn't know that for sure. *Maybe a dime...* He was starting to feel a mild pressure on his lungs, but he knew he still had a minute to figure it all out. He eased the pointer finger of his right hand through the grate to see if he could reach anything. It was a very tight fit, even for his small fingers. He pushed the finger in as far as it would go to see if it was going to reach the spot where he thought he saw the metallic glint just moments before.

Man, no luck! Maybe I can pull the grate up, he thought. Jake pushed his thumb into one of the holes on the grate near his index finger and he gave a hard tug. It didn't budge. He planted his left hand, clutched in a fist holding two coins, on the concrete pool bottom and pushed. He simultaneously gave two more tugs in quick succession, as hard as he could, with his right hand. It just wasn't going to work. He was mildly disappointed that he wouldn't come up with all twelve coins in three dives. *Oh, well, I'll do it in three dives next try,* he commiserated with himself.

Jake tried to pull his right hand free from the grate so that he could swim up to the surface. He realized that he really needed air—there was now some urgency mounting in his lungs.

But his hand didn't move.

It didn't move! He pulled again—nothing!

His thumb and index finger were both stuck.

He began to panic as he felt a very real fear envelope him. His fingers were wedged into the grating—his knuckles were caught—he couldn't pull free. He let go of the coins in his left hand and they silently dropped next to him. With that hand free, he pulled again and again. He twisted his fingers frantically and pulled at them with his free hand. He thought he felt them loosen, but it was just a trick of the situation.

Jake looked up desperately towards the surface hoping that Grandpa would see him, see that he needed help. Nobody was there—only the shimmery reflection of his grandparents' back yard.

His panic was reaching a climax. Three things went through his mind during the next few seconds...

First, he was sorry that he had gotten himself in this trouble and wasn't safe.

Second, he thought that he was going to cry, if that was possible under water.

Even though he felt manic, as if he might go crazy, he was beginning to slow down and his movements were now lethargic. Every now and then, his body twitched uncontrollably as he tried to hold out, find that last bit of additional oxygen in his burning lungs.

The third and final thing that went through Jake's mind before his body yielded to the urge to inhale was that he loved his mom and his dad very, very much.

After that he opened his mouth, water entered his body, and the world went black.

~~~~~

Samantha and I pulled into my parents' driveway and parked in the empty spot right next to the front door. I didn't see my parents' vehicles, but that didn't mean anything—they could be in the garage.

"Well, the absence of cops is good," Samantha said, but it was just chatter. My intuition had been pervasive—Samantha had succumbed easily and inherited my own unwelcome feelings that something wasn't right. She had tried calling my parents multiple times without luck, which only made both of us more apprehensive.

I grunted. My feeling quickly escalated from bad to horrible—almost unbearable. My insides churned and my peripheral vision disappeared as my focus increased. I jumped out of the vehicle, trotting toward the front door with my keys in hand. Samantha was right there beside me, right hand on my left shoulder, as the front door opened.

"Hello?" I hollered into the silent house. "Jake? Mom...Dad?"

I moved to the left, into the kitchen area, while Samantha moved right towards the bedrooms. We both hollered. Only silence answered us. My wife and I converged in the living room and I noticed the video game controllers askance on the tabletop.

"Jack!"

I looked at Samantha. She was walking toward the set of French doors that open to the backyard, concern all over her face. I followed her, saw my dad in his lounger, and scanned the backyard.

"Dad," I said loudly, shouted really, when we stepped out onto the patio. My dad appeared startled, as if from deep sleep. Sam and I started moving toward my father, but we also looked around for Jacob, too. "Where's Jacob?" I asked him as we reached the border of the pool. My dad didn't have time to answer.

Samantha saw him first.

"Oh my God," she moaned, or screamed…I'm not sure which. I looked where she looked, a dark and knowing cloak of dread settling on me.

Years later, I would describe that moment as the culmination of all my worst fears. Nothing prepares parents for the shock of traumatic situations involving their children. Nothing. Firefighters train every day for years for the situations they are thrust into and *still* aren't always ready for what they see; however, they have that training, that muscle memory that they can rely on at a moment's notice. Athletes have it, too.

I saw a shape at the bottom of the pool. It was the saddest thing imaginable, but there wasn't any doubt; it was my son. He wasn't moving.

My muscle memory kicked in then. Except, not from training—but from eleven years of loving Jacob—eleven years of a dad loving his son. That's the muscle memory that guided me.

No more than a second or two had passed even though things felt as if they had slowed down, were not moving, or no longer existed. I didn't take time to remove my shoes or my watch—I didn't even think about those things—I immediately dived into the pool. I stroked my arms harder than I ever had before, and it's overkill, I only needed one stroke, and I was at my son's back, pulling at his underarms. He didn't move.

I tugged harder, but Jake was caught on something. I swam around to face him. My heart stopped when I saw his face—so young—so peaceful. My emotions were bursting inside of me, but I couldn't waste time with anything except getting my son above water. I frantically searched around him and found his hand, his fingers, jammed down into the grating at the bottom of the pool. I grabbed the grating but it didn't budge.

I didn't think about being gentle. I twisted, and I

tugged, and I saw the abrasions on Jake's fingers from my efforts.

Finally, his hand came free. I pushed off from the bottom, holding him, and we exploded through the surface together. I didn't feel his weight at all—he was as light as a feather. I moved quickly to the edge of the pool and pushed his body up while Samantha pulled and we got him out of the water quickly.

"Jake!" Samantha screamed, then, "Help! We need help! He's not breathing!"

I threw myself up and out of the pool and went to Jacob's side. I barely noticed my wife's screaming as I pushed in beside her and leaned in to my son. I saw his face again, and this time it affected me, deep down—he's the most beautiful and important thing in this life—and I almost lost it. I looked down at that sweet face.

"Jake..." I whispered.

He didn't move and I was pretty certain he was not breathing.

Samantha moved over when I started doing chest compressions. I hoped that I was doing them correctly—it'd been a while since my last CPR training. Even then, I wasn't sure I should be doing it because I was never an expert. It's just one of those things that popped up at random times in my life: high school health class; when Jake was a toddler; and at work a few years ago.

"...28...29...30," I counted the compressions and checked quickly to see if he was breathing, but he was not. I tilted Jake's head back, lifted his chin and pinched his nose shut. I gave him three breaths. His chest rose with each, but he didn't start breathing. *Damn it*, I thought to myself, *I was only supposed to give him two breaths!* I cursed myself for not remembering.

I started the next series of chest compressions. My hands appeared enormous on Jake's chest, but I tried to focus. *Press down 1-2 inches per compression. Stay away from that little piece of bone (what was it called?) that's at the end of the breastbone and can potentially be broken.*

"Come on, Jake..." Samantha begged. I couldn't see her, but I heard the tears in her voice. The awful desperate quality...

"...28...29...30," I finished another set of compressions. I placed my face next to Jake's, next to his open mouth. He still wasn't breathing. I gave him mouth-to-mouth again, this time only two breaths. *Is that right?* I pushed a little harder this time when I breathed into my son. His chest rose, fell...rose, fell...but it didn't rise again on its own.

I immediately began another set of chest compressions. I didn't have any idea if I was doing it right anymore. I could only hope. Hope was all that I had left and I didn't know how long I'd have that, but I couldn't stop trying while it was there.

"...28...29...30," I counted quietly, finishing a third set of compressions. I kissed my son's forehead quickly when I leaned down to his face. *Come back to me, buddy.* I turned my head and listened at his mouth. I frowned. I thought I heard something, but I couldn't tell. For a third time I put my mouth to his and tried to give him back his life.

When he started coughing up water I blanched and pulled back, momentarily confused, until I realized that my son was moving again. At that point I didn't know what to do— CPR classes never covered near drowning—not that I remembered. I rolled his body to about a 45-degree angle as he continued to cough and sputter up pool water.

Even though there were still tears coming down her face, my wife was reinvigorated; she was infused with higher purpose. She grabbed a towel from nearby and covered my son while I brought him almost fully onto his side. He was still spitting up a *little* water, but mostly just coughing, and even though he wasn't really moving, I saw that he was breathing, or at least his upper body gave the impression of breathing, which flooded me with relief.

"Can you hear me, buddy? Everything's okay, Jake. Everything is going to be okay if you just stay strong and stay with Mommy and Daddy," I told him. I was vaguely aware of distant sirens as I held my son and talked to him.

Samantha hunkered next to Jake, hugging him, rubbing his arms, and whispering to him. I couldn't hear what she was saying, but I knew the power of motherhood was in every word.

Jacob remained unresponsive to us; however, he was breathing, and I held onto that. I didn't have any idea what to do after CPR so I did nothing. I thought to myself, *I should get up and call an ambulance*, but for the moment I just couldn't let go of Jacob.

I realized the sirens that I heard earlier were getting louder, very loud, and somewhere inside me I knew it was for my son. It had to be.

I didn't know how much time elapsed, but it wasn't very much. Two men, paramedics, appeared in front of me and firmly and quickly asked me questions to assess the situation and determine my son's condition. Their precise mannerisms were comforting in an odd way. I didn't want to release my son and I didn't have to...they wanted me in the ambulance so they could continue questioning me on the way to the hospital.

My wife kissed Jacob before he was removed to the vehicle and she hugged me briefly: "Take care of him, Jack! Take care of him!"

"Okay," I replied, but it was sort of like an out-of-body experience for me. Like I watched myself say it from a place of observation above the scene. In this manner, I also recognized my father standing off to the side, perhaps twenty paces behind my wife. I could see that the Jack down on the ground saw his father but didn't speak to him or acknowledge him. The Billy Leonard on the ground said nothing and quickly averted his eyes from the Jack on the ground. Then I saw Jack jump into the back of the ambulance, the doors closed, and it zipped away with the last of the afternoon.

~~~~~

The ride to the hospital and the first few hours that followed were a blur.

I remembered watching my son, his small, pale angelic face, as we rushed through Houston to the background music of emergency sirens. Thankfully, it was muted inside the vehicle. Flashing lights danced in the periphery of my vision. The paramedic asked me questions while he worked at stabilizing Jacob. *Oh, Jacob...be strong, buddy.*

Our entry into the hospital emergency room was loud and fast like the beginning of a horse race. I moved to follow the paramedics as they wheeled my son into back rooms with closed doors, but people barred my way. I made a small scene when they told me that I would have to go to the waiting area. I couldn't explain it, but I felt like they were conspiring against me and I didn't understand why I was being kept from Jacob. I may have pushed somebody—I'm not sure. They were nice to me anyway—as nice as you can be when engaged in a contest with an agitated, desperate father.

A lone doctor stayed with me for a few minutes. He attempted to talk me back from the ledge, so to speak, but it didn't work. *"The situation is uncertain, but you must remain calm, Sir."* Right. His words were delivered kindly enough, but they still caused me pain. Everything caused pain. The emotional sponge inside me had been wrung dry.

I resigned myself to not being in the back with my son and started pacing the room. *Keep him safe, God,* I prayed inwardly. Samantha and I were what you would call non-practicing Christians. We were good people. We tried to contribute to society in a positive way and we established a solid, moral path for our son. But, if our Christianity were a head of lettuce it would be turning brown—neglected— abandoned and forgotten in the refrigerator. We prayed and attended church only infrequently. My last prayer prior to this one was probably at Easter.

An interminable amount of time later, the double-doors banged open.

"Jack! Oh, Jack!" I turned and Samantha rushed into my arms. I squeezed her, hugged her, maybe too hard, but it was extra relief to my pained heart. Only a few paces behind Samantha, my mom rushed into the room, too. She didn't wait for Sam and me to separate, she grabbed us both in a hug of her own. Between the three of us there weren't any dry eyes.

"Where is Jake? He's okay, isn't he?" my wife pleaded. More tears sprang to her eyes and I felt my own, watery and hot. There was a bulgy feeling in my forehead when I replied to Samantha.

"They aren't sure. His vital signs haven't stabilized and he is still unresponsive," I began, pausing now and then, forcing myself to speak calmly. "Since nobody knows how long he was under water, they don't have any starting point to make any guesses." The thought of Jake under the water was unbearable. I paused again. I rubbed my forehead. My eyes felt as if they were expanding, painfully, to an unknown limit.

"They feel positive about his vitals. They think he is going to stabilize soon. But..." I stopped and looked at the floor. I didn't think I could say the rest and I wasn't sure I should...except that Samantha deserved to know, too.

"But, what, Jack?" Samantha asked.

"They won't know until he's conscious, but he might have *brain damage*..." I gritted my teeth when I said the last two words. *Brain damage—my Jake, my little Jake.* I became aware of a low noise in the room. It was me. I was moaning, a horrible sound, soft, but penetrating, like an animal's death cry. I was at my limit. I always thought I was pretty tough—a strong guy— but I was nothing.

"Okay, Jack. Okay. Shhh..." Samantha took my head and pushed it gently to her shoulder. She *has* to be as destroyed as I am, yet *she* is somehow comforting *me*. This restored the smallest modicum of strength when I needed it most and gave me some solace. She was an amazing woman.

Samantha led me over to a bank of chairs along the wall and we collapsed into two of them, still holding each other. Samantha was on my right side. My mother sat down on my left and put her arm around my shoulders.

"Oh, Mom..." my voice broke a little bit. My emotions were raw and I was certain I had never been stretched any thinner.

"Shhh...Jacky. Shhh..." my mom whispered soothingly.

The three of us huddled together and waited.

Chapter 10
August 10th and 11th, 2001

"Jack..."

"Mmm..."

...a few seconds later...

"Jack..."

"Mmm..."

...a few more seconds later...

"Jack!"

"Yeah?"

"It's time."

...*Why is Samantha waking me up...she knows I had a tiring week at work...what's it time for anyway...*

"It's time?! Oh my God! Are you serious?"

"Of course I'm serious, Jack."

I jumped up from the bed like my boxer shorts were on fire. I feinted toward the door then turned toward the closet. I looked over at Samantha. She hadn't moved—she lay unmoving—watching me.

"But...you're not due for another four days," I said lamely.

"I know, but it's time, I'm having regular contractions."

"Whoa...oh, man." I wasn't feeling so good about this.

"It's okay. The contractions are still pretty far apart."

"But...we didn't choose the name...not for sure, yet..."

"I don't think he's going to wait for a name."

"Right."

"How about you throw on some clothes and get everything ready. I'll go freshen up...*mmm*..." she peeked at her watch. "We'll meet at the front door in 15 minutes."

"Okay. Got it. I'll get everything ready," I told her.

That was twenty minutes ago.

"Jack! What are you doing?" Samantha asked loudly.

She sounded concerned, but not overly excited; she was still in control.

"I'm trying to find your hospital bag." My voice cracked and hit a high note, as if I were a teenager instead of 26 years old. I was rapidly losing all semblance of control. My excitement was in overdrive.

Composed and patient: "Jack...it's right there in the coat closet."

Freaking out (a little bit): "Where? Where?" I swatted things to the side, pushed here, and prodded there, in my search for the bag.

There I was, the guy you see in all the romantic comedies, dancing and bumbling around like a fool because *it's time*. Coming soon to a theater near you: *This baby will be born on the carpet!* starring Jack Leonard. You can catch the lovable, incompetent Jack in his other blockbuster hit, too: *Can't get anything right!*

Just when I thought I might completely lose it, I saw the bag. It was right in front of me. Not *sort of* right in front of me...but dead center; it was right there.

"Well, if it were a snake it would have bit me..." I mumbled to myself. I reached over calmly and picked up the large duffel bag which was crammed with assorted sleepwear, snacks, books, and our good camera.

"Jack?"

I smiled to myself. Just like that I had regained some of my composure. *Some.* Enough.

"Be right there, Sam."

We drove to the hospital. At Samantha's insistence, I didn't speed. Not much, anyway. She used our cell phone and made the calls we had planned on making: my parents; my sister; and my best friend, Scott. Then Samantha called her best friend, Raquel. We had pre-programmed them in the cell phone, so she just used speed dial to knock them out: one, two, three, four. Sadly, there was no one in Samantha's family to call since her parents were deceased.

We made it to the hospital with time to spare. Our admittance was a piece of cake; we had pre-filled all of our forms. Samantha was in high spirits and her contractions were still spaced well apart. We had no horror stories or close calls. I wouldn't have a harrowing, *near miss* story to share with people and I was fine with that.

Katie was the first to arrive on the scene. She rushed in, full of energy, all smiles for Samantha. She had a vase with flowers and balloons. Katie hugged Samantha and whispered into her ear. It made me smile to myself. She was one hundred percent Katie: one hundred percent prepared.

Scott was next. He was calm and confident, full of jokes, a little bit bigger than life. He brought with him a teddy bear dressed in a Tennessee Titans jersey. I laughed in spite of myself. We were both Houston Oilers fans as kids. When Bud Adams took the team away from Houston, Scott decided he'd continue to be a fan of the Tennessee team with Houston roots. While, I vowed to pray for their losses until my last dying breath.

"For young Scott Leonard," he joked, setting the teddy bear down next to Samantha.

"Stupid Titans," I replied.

"Thank you, Scott," Samantha smiled. He gave her a peck on the cheek, and smirked at me as if to say…*nanny-nanny-boo-boo*.

Like Katie, Scott was true to himself *and* true to us. He had never let me down—ever.

I tossed an arm around his shoulder, "Thanks, buddy."

"Don't get all weepy on me, now, Texas Jack. You've got a lady bringing your kid into the world soon."

"True…true…"

A female doctor came in to check on Samantha, so Katie and Scott stepped outside into the hallway.

"How are you feeling tonight, Mrs. Leonard? Are you ready to have a baby?"

"I'm okay…I *guess* I'm ready."

She wasn't our regular doctor, but we had met her as part of a hospital orientation visit and right away we liked her.

"We've called your doctor, but he might not make it. He's helping with an emergency situation at another hospital. But, no worries...I've done this a thousand times. Now...I'm just going to take a peek and see how things look, okay?" She put on gloves and went about checking my wife *down there*, which always freaked me out a little bit.

"Good. It looks like you're at about six to seven centimeters of cervical dilation. You've been progressing steadily. There's no way to be absolutely sure, but it looks like you'll deliver in the next few hours."

"Great. Thank you."

"Of course. Oh, and just double-checking...you didn't want an epidural?"

"Umm, I don't think so..." Samantha said.

"It's up to you. Once you get too far...there is no going back."

"I'm fine. I told myself I would do this naturally."

"Okay. I'll come by again soon to check on you."

The doctor left the room and Katie and Scott rushed back in before the door had the chance to close all the way. I gave Samantha a quick hug. She was becoming a little withdrawn so I figured that she was feeling things a little more.

"Everything good in the hood?" Scott strolled up to the bed.

"Dude...you missed it...the doctor was talking about dilated cervixes."

Scott shuddered. "That's disgusting, brother."

"Yes," I agreed. "Very."

"Jack!" Katie said in her peppy-yet-scolding voice.

"Oh, it's okay." Samantha smiled.

"I've got the best lady ever," I told my wife. "I love you with all my heart."

"I love you, too..." she said.

Katie, the fountain of perpetual happiness: "Awww! I

love y'all!"

"Yep. You guys are something special. Especially you, Samantha. Jack's a little bit special because of his association with you. Otherwise, he's just sort of average really."

"Thanks, bro. Love you, too." We were accustomed to Scott's little rants.

The three of us huddled around Samantha and she seemed okay...for the time being. We were all there for her, providing comfort and stability, each in our own different ways.

Every so often, at regular intervals, Sam would have some contractions, and we would catch a glimpse of just how serious this situation was about to be. I tried to be rock-solid for her during those moments, holding her hand, wiping her forehead, and fetching her ice chips. How ice chips could provide any relief to anything was a mystery to me, but I did as I was told.

Katie, just by being herself, brought cheer to the room. She sang songs, laughed, clapped her hands, and offered consistent verbal reassurances to everyone.

Scott's presence was a testament to his love for the Leonard family. I could tell that the contractions were something he wasn't especially comfortable with. I understood where he was coming from—if it weren't my wife on the bed, I would have bolted. But it would have taken the Jaws of Life to remove him from the room. He was with us no matter what.

A few hours passed and things slowly, and surely, escalated. The female doctor...*what was her name?*... came and checked on us again, smiling reassuringly, and told us that it would probably be soon.

I started to wonder if my parents would make it in time when the door opened, and presto, there they were.

"Samantha! Jack!" My mother burst into the room. She was glowing—eager to have a grandchild—and looked ten years younger. She immediately gave Samantha a hug and began speaking quietly with her.

"Jack." My name sounded more like a firecracker than a

greeting when it came out of my father's mouth. He was wearing his standard uniform, blue jeans and a button-up shirt, but it was tucked, and he had a sports coat on, too. Billy Leonard strolled into the room behind Lainey and I realized that he had been smiling since they opened the door. He was holding his head up high, too. *The old man is really excited,* I thought. *He's really excited about being a grandfather...who would have thought!*

He gave me a man-hug and then walked over to Samantha's bedside where he tipped his head once and said, "Samantha. I hear that my grandson is itchin' to pay us a visit." He smiled at her and winked.

"He sure is, Dad. Not sure how much longer he's going to wait." She pressed down with her palms into the mattress on either side of her, which had become her non-verbal cue that a contraction was firing off, so I made my way to her side and held her hand.

"Well, well. We are about to continue the family name! Speaking of names, did you guys settle on a first name yet?"

His question caught us off guard. It was true that we had been deliberating on names for, oh, nine months. We had the short list of first names...five to be exact...but we hadn't picked *the one* yet.

"We haven't decided, officially. But, we will soon," Samantha said. She didn't give up any more information.

We all laughed a little bit at that. Soon he would be here whether or not he had a name. I leaned down and gave Samantha a quick kiss and she whispered in my ear, "We'll know it when we see him."

"Okay."

My dad motioned to me and Scott, then pulled us aside. "You know, back in my day, I wasn't allowed in the delivery room with your mother. In some ways, that was nice...no responsibility. But, I know it's going to be to Samantha's favor that you are in there, Jack. Scott...sure it will be that way for you, too, when the time comes." He was completely sober, yet behaving with the light, bubbly air and mannerisms that I associated with Drunk Billy. It was weird. Maybe the years of drinking had genetically altered him, transforming him gradually into Drunk Billy 24 hours a day. I didn't know.

As the contractions got closer and closer, the doctor came in and told us it was time to switch rooms. I struggled to remember her name as we rolled Samantha into one of the delivery rooms. I wanted to be able to communicate with her when things were going down.

~~~~~

Everyone had cleared out of the delivery room an hour earlier. Except for Samantha and I, in full scrubs, of course. The doctor and nurse had stepped out, but were due back any moment. Samantha's eyes were closed. The last hour had been pretty rough for Samantha as the pains of delivery washed over her in waves.

I was feeling jammed up inside. My emotions were dancing around, confused, and I decided it would be a good moment to share some of what I was feeling with her. I put my hand into hers and our fingers intertwined, naturally it seemed, like they were made as a single unit and only separated afterwards. I leaned down close to her.

"I love you, Samantha," I told her. She didn't open her eyes, but I continued. "The first time I saw you, well, I just knew. Do you remember that? I never thought I would meet the girl of my dreams at a *Nirvana* concert. Right? You emerged from a sea of plaid shirts, tan and beautiful, like you were dropped down there from heaven or something.

"I knew we were going to be something great. When I saw you it was like I already knew you. Some sort of predestined match, if you believe in that sort of thing.

"And, well, I believe in it. Because of you." I paused. I thought I might cry if I kept it up, so I just decided to keep it short. "We're something great, Samantha. I love you."

"Mmm..." Samantha moaned. Her eyes were closed.

"Ha ha...do you remember when you asked me if I had something against shirts? That was funny. I laughed myself to sleep that night thinking about that."

Sam's eyes fluttered open then. She focused on me and I smiled at her. I thought she was going to respond to everything that I had been telling her, maybe return the sentiments.

Instead she reached out and grabbed the collar of my

shirt. Her grip was surprisingly strong and she pulled my face close to hers.

"Get. The. Epidural." She said to me.

"Uh...okay. Okay." *We'll finish that talk later,* I thought as I ran to the door and opened it. Female Doctor was there, reaching out to where the door had been, to push it open.

"Uhh, hi, um, Doctor. My wife, Samantha, she'd like the epidural now."

"Mr. Leonard, it may be too late. Let me check."

I went back to my wife's side and waited while the doctor did another one of her *checks* on the nether regions of my wife.

"Mr. Leonard, your wife is dilated almost ten centimeters. It's too late to administer the epidural...she's going to deliver very soon."

Samantha's fingers dug into my forearm—hard.

I guessed she had heard the doctor.

The next hour may have been the longest hour in the history of time. It was hard on Samantha, but she's a fighter and drew from a reserve of energy that I didn't think was possible. I gave her what little strength I had, too. In the end, after a lot of breathing—and cursing—the doctor moved into position between Samantha's legs.

I noted the doctor, the quarterback, had good hand placement and was communicating well with the center, Samantha. I prayed that there wouldn't be a shotgun snap and my prayer was answered; they used the classic under-center snap. The doctor got the baby with both hands and a firm grip and made the play—quarterback sneak—and score!

I wanted to cheer. I think I did cheer; I'm not sure. It was the most beautiful play these eyes had ever seen. I looked down at my wife: sweaty, disheveled, and obliterated. But, happy! Oh, wow, she never looked more beautiful to me and I kissed her forehead. Then I kissed her forehead again. And again.

Then we heard the baby cry. I thought my heart might

stop.

"Hey, guys…you've got a beautiful baby boy here."

Female Doctor called me over for the ceremonial umbilical cord cutting. I took the *scissors* and gave them a squeeze. It was weird, like when you accidentally chew on gristle next to a rib; that's how it felt to my hands. It didn't immediately cut, so I repeated the action, and it finally did. I was amazed and a little horrified at the same time.

In no time the baby was in Samantha's arms and she was cooing at her creation. I noticed that Sam's legs were still in the crazy looking stirrups, but she didn't seem to mind. You could say she was completely absorbed in something a little more important.

The doctor and nurse were bustling around the room, doing whatever they do after a baby is born. Female Doctor came back and settled in *down there* and started sewing things back together.

"Hey, Doc…maybe you can put an extra stitch in there?" My wife groaned audibly, but hey, I couldn't resist it. I had been planning that joke for months and Female Doctor wasn't going to stop me from what might be my only chance to ever use that joke.

"There's an extra fee for that, that insurance doesn't cover," Female Doctor replied. I stared at her dumbly for a second before she looked up from her handicraft and said, "Gotcha."

I laughed then and looked at Samantha who just gave me a tired smile. I was pretty lucky to have found someone who put up with all of my shenanigans.

"Jack?"

"Yeah, honey?"

"Jacob. He looks like a Jacob to me," she said. I looked at the baby in her arms and touched his little tiny nose with my finger. He had one hand wrapped tightly around my wife's pinky and the other held close to his chest, like he was playing poker and didn't want you to see his cards.

"Hey, Jacob," I told him. "Welcome to the family."

~~~~~

When I went out to the waiting area everyone looked up at me expectantly and I couldn't keep the smile off my face.

"Hey, everybody. Samantha's doing great...and in a few minutes, we'll go down to the nursery...so you can meet Jacob."

"Congrats, brother!" Scott jumped up and we did the one-hand-grasp-then-man-hug deal.

My mom and sister followed right on his heels, hugging me, too. "Jacob's such a wonderful name!" Katie chirped. She was crying and smiling. My mom was, too.

My dad followed next with a bear hug. "I'm proud of you, Son. Congratulations."

"Thanks, Dad."

We visited the nursery and Jacob Thomas Leonard was right up front.

"He looks just like you..."

"Oh, he's a big guy..."

"He looks like Samantha, too..."

"Jacob's a good name, but Scott...that's a great name..."

"Wow, he's got a lot of hair..."

"You guys do good work..."

Female Doctor found us and let me know that Samantha was in a different room now. I thanked her profusely, referring to her as "Doctor" and "Ma'am," but I noticed the small lettering on her name tag said Dr. Alicia Stone. *Ah-ha!*

Peeling away from the window with smiles and laughter, one by one, we made our way through the hallway to my wife: the world's newest mother. I poked my head into the room and Samantha looked up at me and smiled.

"Is it okay for us to come in?" I asked.

"Sure..."

I opened the door wide and we flooded the little room.

The girls immediately went to Samantha's side while the men stayed back with heads held high. I was tempted to beat on my chest like a caveman.

"Hey, that reminds me..." my dad said, pulling a pouch from the inside pocket of his sports coat, handing it to me. "Son, as you requested...the *Cue*-bans."

I reached inside and pulled out the cigars I had asked my dad to pick up. He was really resourceful for the strangest things. He had some secret supplier, for illegal Cuban cigars, he wouldn't name.

I handed cigars over to Scott and my dad and we all stood back, smelling and admiring them.

"Team Leonard! We just got another member on Team Leonard," my dad proclaimed smiling, and put an arm around me.

"And Scott!" Scott added.

"Scotty, my boy, you *are* part of Team Leonard," my dad told him with a wink.

I looked around the room at everyone present. It was the best group of people I had ever known—my family—Team Leonard.

Chapter 11
Thursday, August 9th, 2012

After midnight, the double-doors at the end of the room finally stopped swinging so damned frequently and remained closed more often than not. Patients and medical staff moved around with decreasing regularity as evening became the middle of the night, and the middle of the night became morning. For the most part, we sat listlessly as patients with different traumas and ailments moved in and around us. It was like we were starring in one of those movies where the main character is sitting still while the world zooms around her leaving tracers, streaks of color, that indicate rapid passage.

We were the immobile lead characters in that scenario. In movies it's interesting, or amusing, but in real life it isn't.

My mother, my wife, and I didn't speak much—words were hard to come by—but, we watched and hoped and waited. We mutually consoled each other with the intangible force of our hopes and our presence.

The squeak of the double-doors didn't fail to get my attention every time they were opened. It was a crazy, repeating sequence of minor events: telltale squeak, my head lifting, *whump* of the doors shutting, realization that it's not about Jake, then my head lowering. I longed for definitive news of my son. The physician attending Jake, Dr. Alvin Nichols, had given us small updates. Well, that is if you consider an unchanging situation to be updatable. I didn't blame him, yet, his not knowing anguished me. It was simply hell and I was growing tired of it all: the waiting and not knowing.

Dozens of people passed, each wrapped up in their own worries and troubles. I repeatedly looked at them, hoping they were someone sent to bring me good news, and I was repeatedly disappointed. They were just other people with their own predicaments. They carried crying children or followed loved ones into adjoining rooms. Blood, breaks, tears, and frustration reigned supreme here and nothing happened quickly.

With so much time on my hands, it was inevitable that I play out the events of the previous afternoon and evening multiple times. Reliving the experience was the last thing I wanted to do, but I couldn't help myself. They say idle hands lead to the devil's work, but what about the idle mind? What does it do?

I rewound the events and hit play again.

We departed Galveston in the late afternoon, bound for my parents' house. We checked the house quickly then went to the backyard, where my dad was asleep...

(*Passed out*)

...and that's when the nightmare really begins.

Obviously he was asleep in a lounge chair next to the pool, but where was my dad when Jake needed him? Why wasn't he awake and watching Jake? And...where was he now? I found myself sitting on an emotional fence with worry and fear on one side and anger and confusion on the other. Thinking about my dad threatened to push me off the fence towards anger and fear.

What made me angriest is that I suspected (knew) that my dad was drinking. He hadn't simply fallen asleep—he had passed out. He had passed out and allowed his grandson to drown...

(*But Jake is alive*)

...to drown, to go unnoticed, at the bottom of a pool. It was more than unsettling; it was unbelievable, unfathomable, beyond reason, and heartbreaking.

Except it wasn't, I thought. *That's my dad.*

He had been drinking my entire life. Heck, he had been drinking almost *his* entire life. There were, literally, only a handful of days I could recall my father not drinking. My graduations and school events didn't make that list. Not that he was embarrassingly liquored up—he really did have a legendary tolerance—but a blood test would probably have shocked any physician.

My wedding didn't make the cut either. My dad was *feeling no pain* before we reached the church that afternoon, but he didn't lose control. Again, he went to his little happy drunk place and plateaued there.

Don't even think about football games making the list. They were some of the worst, at least in regard to volume of booze consumed. *Billy Leonard and the Case of the Burned Couch* was a recurring non-mystery.

The same thing went for Katie—never a sober moment for Billy Leonard—occasion be damned. Girls react differently than boys to alcoholic parents. I thought of my father's behavior as a natural, masculine response to the environment. Katie approached him often as a scolding mother might...lovingly, but with a scowl. I don't think he ever noticed that. He'd just open another beer.

We all made adjustments in our individual lives, allowances if you will, for William Leonard and his habits.

We didn't like it, but we all accepted it, and really, acceptance says it's okay.

So...was it our fault?

I couldn't accept that, but in a way, it was true. If I had put my foot down and confronted my dad, I mean really laid out an ultimatum about his drinking, then Jacob might be okay right now. Maybe I was as much to blame for all of this as my dad. Or maybe none of us were to blame. I didn't know.

I knew my dad loved his grandson. That was never in question; however, as an adult he had never behaved responsibly and now he had endangered Jacob, who meant more than anything on Earth to me.

I shuddered and let out a long sigh. The clock on the wall said that it was 4am—I had been killing myself thinking about it for hours. In the end I just wanted my son to be okay.

Samantha had slid to the opposite side of her chair,

away from me, and it looked like she might be sleeping. My mother had peeled away from me in the opposite direction. We looked like a human banana.

Over the next hour the hospital began to wake up. People entered sporadically, and passed by, leaving the waiting room smelling faintly of soap, shampoo, aftershave, and lotions. They all wore scrubs. It was disconcerting to me that all of them were going on normally with their lives, while my son was languishing in a back room somewhere.

I noticed that we were the only people left that weren't hospital employees. At some point in the morning everyone else had moved on.

"Mr. Leonard," Dr. Nichols called softly, pushing through the double-doors with a *squeak* and *whump*. My wife and mother immediately stirred into life, leaving me to wonder if they had gotten any real sleep or just morsels of microsleep.

"Doctor," I said, standing up hopefully. Samantha stood, too. He walked up to us quickly and placed one hand on my shoulder and one on Sam's. I couldn't read his face.

"Mr. and Mrs. Leonard," he said somewhat softly. "I have a little more information for you now, but before we get too deep into the technical side of things, the good news is that, for the most part, your son has stabilized. His vital signs have all returned to a, well, a mostly normal range, all things considered."

I think that Sam, my mother, and I all exhaled simultaneously. The release of tension was palpable. "What exactly does that mean, Doc? Can we see him?" I asked.

"Well, this situation is not black and white, Mr. Leonard. While I feel that your son has made it through the worst of the immediate dangers, the situation is still very, very complicated."

"Complicated?" Samantha said. She looked from me to Dr. Nichols expectantly.

"Your son," the doctor began, "he is stable...but, he hasn't awakened. Not yet."

"He's in a coma?" Samantha asked, cutting him off.

"Well, yes, but that isn't something you should feel good or bad about at this point. Right now, this very instant, stabilizing him has been the most important thing. And he is stable.

"Since his body is telling us, through those stable vital signs, that it has the strength and ability required to stay alive, now we can investigate and run more tests to determine the extent, if any, of any damage that his *near* drowning may have caused. You shouldn't be afraid of his comatose status—that is neither good or bad—and actually somewhat normal for this situation. Just think of it as sleeping and recuperating for now. Okay?" He looked at us, and we nodded our heads.

"So, we have weathered a difficult part of this storm, and things look promising, but we aren't in the clear yet. There is still much we don't know. And, that's why we have to run tests. More than that, we have to wait. Time is what will give us all the answers. The absolute, most important thing you can do, that we can all do, is remain positive." Again his eyes traveled from Sam to me. Again we nodded.

"In addition to the more serious problems we discussed, he did have comparatively minor injuries to his right hand. He had many minor lacerations and several of the joints in his right hand were dislocated; there were some torn tendons; and one of his fingers is fractured."

I grimaced and felt sick—I had caused those injuries.

"Mr. Leonard," he said, interpreting my reaction and making extended eye contact with me, "there is no doubt that you saved Jacob's life. Make no mistake about that. You. Saved. His life. Because of your actions, we're here right now discussing his recovery. I think it's important for you to hear that again, and that you give yourself that. I mention these minor injuries only to make sure you are informed—a broken finger is worth the alternative." He continued to hold my eyes when he finished speaking. I felt the return of some inner strength that had been faltering. Samantha's arm reached around my shoulders and squeezed. I think she felt it, too.

"Drowning is the number one cause of accidental deaths in the United States. Because we are a large city, and because we are so close to the coast here in Houston, we have an experienced staff in regard to near-drowning cases. Your son will be getting exceptional care here.

"So far it looks like there will be little or no sustained damage to Jacob's lungs. Jacob experienced what we call laryngospasm, or a spasm in his larynx, which resulted in the glottis closing."

"Glottis?" I asked.

"Yes, I'm sorry...it's just the opening to the larynx. That closure of the glottis, in the case of your son, is technically what triggered asphyxiation, or suffocation. This reduced the amount of water which entered his lungs. When you are under the water for an extended period, this doesn't mean much, but for Jacob I think it's good and I believe that it has helped during your resuscitation actions and it's helping now.

"The bad news is that we don't know how long he was under the water. The oxygen depravity suffered...knowing how long his body went without air...would give us the most insight into what we can expect. And we just don't know that."

"Can you estimate?" my wife asked.

Dr. Nichols pursed his lips for a moment. "If I had to guess, which I don't like to do because of the unknowable nature of this situation, I would say that it was somewhere between three and six minutes. On the 3-minute end of that spectrum, the low number would account for his recovery so far. Successful resuscitation. Strengthening vitals. Historically, in these situations, the less time spent under water, the better the chances of a full recovery.

"Going toward the 6-minute end of the spectrum, well...while I don't think we would see what we have, it would account for his being unresponsive. Comatose. These conditions are more likely when the various parts of the body are deprived of oxygen for an extended period.

"And, of course, I don't mean to frighten you, but the tests we need to run will give us a good foundation for assessing brain activity."

There it was, not that he meant to frighten us: *Jake may have suffered brain damage.*

"I know that isn't something you want to hear. But, you need to be prepared for it. Statistically speaking, there's a chance that some damage has been done. There might not be anything wrong, or it could be minor." He made eye contact with us and I could see that his bright, green eyes were filled with emotion when he added, "Or it could be more substantial."

Samantha and I traded off and I put my arm around her shoulders and squeezed. I was exhausted and I knew she must be, as well. My mother was hanging in there, too. We were all trying to stay strong.

"It's natural to be upset, but please," the doctor pleaded, "...do try to be positive and keep your spirits up...for each other *and* for Jacob," he said. It was as if he read our minds...or maybe it was his experience with such matters. "Do you have any questions before we go see your son?"

"No, Doctor," my wife answered for us.

Dr. Alvin Nichols nodded his head and smiled softly. "Of course. Please follow me."

~~~~~

We walked down the hallway toward Jacob's room. The smell of disinfectants and cleaners were comforting in a way, but they were also unpleasant—similar to cheap perfume—barely concealing the blood, fluids, and other noxious transients that were frequently guests here.

This section of the hospital seemed particularly dismal. There was an absence of windows, at least as far as I could see; therefore, there wasn't any natural light. The disproportionate amount of fluorescent lighting left everything blanketed in a garish, off-white hue. There was a pervasive colorlessness offset only by the glint of chrome instruments, green hospital scrubs, and a hallway dotted with faux walnut doors. At first glance, there wasn't much comforting here, only a callous, cold place of business.

Dr. Nichols stopped abruptly in front of the door on our right. "I know that you'll want to touch, or hug, your son, and that's fine. But, it's important that you exercise care. Be very careful not to displace the IVs. We have him on an antibiotic right now to prevent pneumonia, which is very common in these situations. He is also being fed through his IV. And, of course, please keep some distance from his right hand even though we have it set and stabilized. It should be fine, but you can never be too careful," he said. "Okay? All ready?"

We nodded our mutual assent, and my heart felt like it was moving higher into my chest, into my throat, making it almost impossible to swallow or breathe. Dr. Nichols opened the door to our son's room.

~~~~~

It was bad, but not as bad as I had imagined.

In the waiting room, where time stood still, my mind had tortured me relentlessly overnight and into this morning. My visions of Jacob were *Grimm's Tales* quality. Unclean surgeons using archaic tools to operate on my son while his blood emptied into buckets. My son: bruised, beaten, clothed in filthy rags. The hallways echoing with harsh laughter.

It was none of that. The mind can play cruel jokes at the most inopportune times.

Jake was in his bed, nearly in the center of the room. The cold glare of the lights did nothing for his sickly pallor. He didn't look outwardly healthy, but there was an underlying vitality that I could feel more than see. I found myself immediately overcome by contradictory feelings: sadness and sympathy for the helpless child on the bed that was my only son and who had done nothing to deserve this; yet, I also felt relief...his heart was beating and there was the unspoken promise of life in his small form.

There were tubes running from his arms to a machine of the sort that you see in all television hospital dramas, which tracked the beat of his heart. It steadily issued soft, rhythmic beeps...and nothing ever sounded so sweet to my ears.

It hadn't even been 24 hours since I last saw Jake, but it felt like years. He looked smaller to me, but surely that was my mind, continuing to play tricks on me.

"Hello, Jacob. Mommy loves you so much," Samantha cooed into his ear.

I walked to the other side of the hospital bed while my mother took up post alongside Samantha. I nearly forgot the doctor's warning and I reached for his hand, but stopped myself at the last second...his little hand was bandaged and splinted.

That happened when I pulled his hand from the drain, I

thought. I felt bad about doing it, but...I was also pretty sure that it was the fastest way to get him out of the water. Maybe the only way.

Instead of grabbing his hand, I leaned in and ran my hand through his hair, careful not to bump anything.

"Hey, buddy." It was something I had been doing since he was a toddler. *Hey, buddy...*then the quick ruffle of the hair. I used to sometimes sniff his hair and make jokes about how he smelled like a puppy. Around the time Jake turned nine he informed me that it would be *inappropriate* to pursue that type of behavior in front of his friends. *Such an amazing, funny little guy,* I thought.

"What are you thinking about, Jack?" Sam asked me.

"What?"

"Just now," she said. "You were sort of smiling."

"Oh. I guess I was just thinking about how I used to smell his hair sometimes and say that he smelled like a little puppy."

Her eyes crinkled and she smiled, "I forgot about that."

"Most of the time I was just joking, but every now and then, when his little head would get sweaty playing outside...well, *sometimes* he really did smell like a little doggy."

Samantha and my mom chuckled softly. I did a little bit, too.

"In a good way," I clarified. "Just our sweaty little guy, always up to something..."

"Yep."

"Yeah..." I trailed off thinking about Jacob. An image of him from a few years back popped into my head. He was laughing while we played catch in the snow. The game became that I would throw him the ball, he would run with it, and I would tackle and tickle him. We must have repeated that 50 times and he never tired of it. Throw, catch, tackle, tickle—just like that.

"He's your buddy," Samantha said and smiled, bringing me back to the present. Her smile was uncharacteristically tinged with sadness. "Jacob's going to be fine."

"He has to be," I responded.

My mother squeezed Samantha's shoulders and looked between us. "He will be," she said very matter-of-factly, settling the matter.

~~~~~

"Jack...can you go get us some breakfast?" Samantha asked. "Or, lunch, I guess? I know you don't want to leave, but..." she trailed off.

I looked at her, startled, then down at my watch. We had been in Jacob's hospital room all morning and it was half past twelve o'clock. It was difficult to imagine that 24 hours ago Samantha and I had been eating shrimp on a pier in Galveston. Eating hadn't crossed my mind since then—wasn't even a consideration—though my stomach grumbled at the thought of food.

"Okay."

"If anything happens I'll call you right away, okay?"

"Okay...please." I nodded, then stood up and stretched. Bones cracked and I felt several minor aches that weren't usually there. "You'd think that hospitals would have windows," I grumbled. "I would think it would be good for the patients." It was impossible to tell how much time passed when the intensity of the lights never changed. Samantha glanced around and nodded her head in agreement. My mother just looked thoughtful.

"Jacky, do you think you can drive me by the house, while you're out?" my mother asked. "I'd like to get a few things...and I think I should be driving separately...just in case we need two cars."

"Sure, Mom. Do you need anything from the house, Sam?"

"No, I'm fine," she said, then hastily added, "Maybe my toothbrush and toothpaste? Whatever you think."

I walked over to Jacob and hugged him lightly—I didn't want to hurt him or disturb his IVs—and whispered, "Be right back, buddy." It may have been my imagination, or wishful thinking, but I thought his color looked better...almost like he had gotten some sun or something. I started to comment about it out loud, but stopped myself. I didn't want to risk jinxing the situation, as silly as that sounded.

I gathered my keys and wallet from the nearby table. My wallet was damp, an unexpected reminder of what had transpired. I decided to hold onto it, instead of returning it to the pocket in my pants, which had dried at some point in the night without me noticing.

"Be back in a little bit," I told Samantha, giving her a quick kiss before my mom and I left the room.

It was dramatically sunny when we reached the lobby of the emergency entrance and stepped outside of the hospital. My senses were almost overcome by the brilliant, pale yellow and my eyes watered. Normally I would have relished in it...now it was only confusing.

"Oh," My mother said and stumbled a little bit.

"Yikes," I agreed. "Did that hospital get their fluorescent lighting schematics from hell? I mean, wow, what's *that* all about?"

"I think they converted this part of the hospital...I don't think it was always for regular patients."

"What do you mean, Mom?"

"I think it was a psychiatric facility in the past—an annex for high-risk patients—to keep them separated. That's why they couldn't have windows. I've heard stories about it."

My ingenious reply: "Oh." I didn't know what to make of that news, but I supposed it didn't really change anything for us.

It took us a few minutes to find the Land Rover. We walked around mumbling things like *that's strange* and *I thought it was right here* before I spotted it on a side street. If there is one certainty in this world, it's the uncertainty of available parking at any Texas hospital.

My mother and I were pretty quiet on the drive back to my parents' house. I can only imagine that, like me, she was trying to sort through it all and put it into perspective. Katie and I had had our moments, and some injuries, but nothing like this. And, believe me, nothing in life prepares you for something of this magnitude happening to your child.

In middle school, high school, and college, Scott and I had lifted weights a lot. Sure, it was expected of everyone on the football team in high school, but we also found that we really enjoyed it. As part of the fervor, we were always trying new supplements advertised to provide the utmost in health and muscle development.

At some point, we stumbled onto these packets of vitamins that purported to provide endless energy, speed up the body's recovery during rest periods, and all the rest of the mumbo jumbo. They had some over-the-top ridiculous name like Mega Monster Vitamins or something. There were six pills in each little foil pouch; however, one of the pills was far larger than the others.

"Horse pill," I told Scott when we cracked open the box of pouches for the first time. "I don't know if a human can ingest that."

"Ah, they wouldn't make it if you couldn't swallow it," was Scott's quick reply. I was doubtful as I held the pill up to the light and studied it. It was nearly as long as a line from the tip of my thumb to the first joint in my thumb! But, logically, Scott had to be right. The mystical *they* that governed the Universe (and produced vitamins) wouldn't sell something that could choke people.

So we opened up our pouches and began knocking back pills. I hesitated briefly before throwing the big one into my mouth with a mouthful of water.

Was it fear? Was my hesitation a catalyst for some type of bodily response that ended ultimately in a narrowed esophagus? I can't answer that with any certainty. What I can tell you is that that pill lodged painfully in my throat. Helpless to do anything about it, that gigantic, son-of-a-bitch of a pill was stuck in my throat within seconds.

Neither the pill nor the water moved anywhere. My heart started racing and I sputtered, choked, and tilted my head forward allowing the water to dribble down my chin and neck. Ragged breaths escaped my throat around the pill as the water made its exodus and the panic subsided slightly when I found I could breathe, but then…

Wham!

Scott whacked me hard on the back while I was completely unaware and that pill fired out of my mouth and across the kitchen floor.

I stood up straight, eyes a little bloodshot from the mini-trauma, and rubbed my hand across the back of my neck. It felt clammy and hot at the same time.

"Whew…thanks, brother," I croaked at Scott.

He grinned and nodded: "No problem."

I took my right hand from the steering wheel and touched my throat as we entered the large, familiar U driveway of my family home. I fought off the phantom pain in my throat. That's what this was…one gigantic pill that life had shoved down my throat, except this time…this time…nobody could whack me on the back and help things along. Only time would tell whether this pill went down…or whether we all choked to death.

~~~~~

My mother turned to me as she pulled her keys from her purse. "I love you, Jacky." She was a good mother, trying to be strong for me, but I could tell she was very sad. We were all hurting inside.

"I know, Mom. I love you, too."

She kept her eyes on me then nodded her head softly. She turned and put her key into the lock on the front door. "Okay. Well, I'm going to be a little while, so I'll just meet you back at the hospital later." She unlocked the door and we walked inside.

"That's fine, Mom. I'm just going to grab some things for Sam and then go grab lunch."

"Okay, dear," she said, leaning over and up, giving me a quick peck on the cheek. Then she moved off to her room and I was suddenly left standing in the entryway, feeling disoriented.

I looked towards the living room, which was half-obscured in darkness. The curtains had been drawn haphazardly, but sunlight was beaming through several openings, casting golden rays of light across the room. One such ray illuminated the coffee table. The video game controllers were there. Images of Jacob, giggling and playing games, floated through my head.

I walked slowly through the living room toward the French doors that opened to the back yard. It was very dark except for where the sun penetrated. When I reached the doors, I drew the curtains aside and opened them as far as my arms would spread.

The sunny, picturesque backyard radiated life and beauty, belying the malevolence of the previous day's events. My mother's flowerbed was a rainbow, half a dozen different flowers reaching proudly toward the sun, blooming colorfully at one end of the yard. The St. Augustine grass was a serene dark green, rich and full, that invited you to walk barefoot in it. The pool...

The pool was a bright turquoise, almost cartoonish in the brilliance of its hue.

I tried not to hate all of it for being so very alive while my son's life was hanging in the balance.

I stepped out onto the patio and walked to the border of the shaded area, next to one of the patio tables, and surveyed it all with a mixture of emotions hard to describe. Hundreds of happy memories were etched here. The discerning side of me knew that the backyard, or the pool, was not to blame for what had happened.

The irrational part of me, however, saw things differently. That dark side wanted to lash out in some pointless way...maybe turn the tables over or throw something. I thought about giving in to the temptation. I had given in to those moments a few times before, but it never ended positively. It probably wouldn't now either.

I let these things roll over and over in my mind like waves crashing onto shore. I started to zone out a little bit. As I stared across the yard, the sun glinted off of something in the patch of grass nearest the deep end of the pool. It drew me out of my thoughts, I moved slightly, and it was gone. I squinted and looked for it...and another flash of dazzling silver came from the grass.

I walked around the pool and stood at the edge of the pavement. Nestled between the fat blades of the St. Augustine grass was the profile of president Franklin D. Roosevelt.

"Hmm."

I reached down and picked up the coin, a dime, one of the shiniest I had ever seen. I vaguely remembered learning about dimes in grade school and how president Roosevelt ended up being the face we see on them.

The story was that Roosevelt had contracted polio in his late thirties while on vacation...I couldn't remember where. He became a staunch supporter for a group that researched possible cures for polio. At one point he called on Americans to support the cause, even if they could just give a dime. The group and cause became known as the March of Dimes. And, after his eventual death, Roosevelt fans requested that his image replace that of Lady Liberty on the dime.

The date on the dime was 2001.

The year Jacob was born, I thought. The superstitious part of me, the part that might perform the same repetitive act before every football game, saw it as a sign of good luck. It made me feel better, infinitesimally better, but better all the same.

I tucked it into my pocket and walked back to the house.

Once inside, I turned and shut the French doors, locking them. I deliberated on whether I should shut the curtains again...or maybe just open all of them to let the light in.

That was when I heard something in the room behind me.

~~~~~

"Jack…" my dad started then stopped. I noticed the pleading in his voice and I made up my mind that I wasn't going to let him off the hook. Not this time.

Billy Leonard was sitting on the small love seat that was tucked away in the darkest corner of the living room. A blanket covered him from feet to chest despite the warmer-than-normal temperature in the house. The perpetually drunk, somewhat charming Billy was gone. In his place there was a gaunt, old man.

I studied him, my mouth set in a hard line.

Sunken, bloodshot eyes looked back at me and met mine. I wondered if he had been drinking.

He looked down and shivered visibly. "Jack…" he started again. "I'm sorry."

"Dad, I don't want to hear it."

"Jack, please, listen to me."

"What, Dad?" I said, raising my voice. "What? What can you possibly want me to hear?"

"Jack…I didn't mean to…"

"How could you let it happen, Dad?" I walked closer to him, never taking my eyes off of him. "Jake means *everything* to me!" I shouted. "How could you do that? How could you treat him like that, with that same…laissez fair, I-don't-give-a-shit attitude that you have about everything else in your life? He deserved better than that, Dad!"

I was just a few feet away from him now. He was no longer making eye contact with me and I noticed that his eyes were wet. This shocked me for a moment—I was raised in a world where *men don't cry* and *only women are emotional*—but it did nothing to crack through the iron resolve I had for this confrontation.

"I love Jake more than anything. Every, single day I am

147

thankful for him. I never knew how good life could be until he was here. Do you get that? Do you?"

"I love him, too, Jack...I can't even sleep thinking about..."

"You can't sleep?" I screamed, incredulous. "You let him drown, Dad! You let him drown! My son was at the bottom of that pool while you snored and SLEPT!" I thundered. "I put up with you my whole life, always drinking, always making mistakes...my graduation, my wedding, parent and teacher conferences...you were drinking when you drove me to take my driver's license test with the sheriffs! Hell, you almost burned our house down...you could have killed all of us!

"But, I never thought it would come to this...that you would treat Jacob with that same disregard...that you would put his life at risk, for what, for beer? So that you could drink beer? He's *your* grandson and he's *my* son!

"You've been careless and irresponsible and I always forgave you. 'Oh, he doesn't mean to be that way,' I would tell people. I made excuses for you. I protected you. My dad didn't do anything wrong.

"When I was young and you weren't there, I wondered if I was the reason that you didn't come home a lot of nights. Other kids told me about things they did with their dad. You know what I did? I lied and made up stories about what we did even though you stayed out drinking all night."

I paused, breathing heavily...I was furious...and I couldn't stop it from coming out. The cork had popped on almost four decades of bottled-up pain, anguish, embarrassment, and shame. Billy Leonard sat, quietly sobbing, not interrupting, and not speaking. It was possibly the first time in his life that he didn't have a reply or make one of his *Billy remarks* that made light of the situation.

"I always stood up for you, Dad. I justified your behavior. I justified it to other people, sure, but I also justified it to myself! You were my dad, and you didn't let people into your world if they didn't accept you. So I accepted you. But...I can't do it anymore. I can't live like this. I can let you hurt me, and that's fine, but I can't let you do this to Jacob. He deserves better than that."

I paused again and shook my head.

"He deserves better than *you*." I said.

My dad's face was ashen—crestfallen—when I turned and walked to the front door. My mother was standing silently in the hallway and I could tell by the look in her eyes that she had witnessed everything. Since there was nothing to say—I said nothing—merely nodded to her as I opened the front door and left. I wondered, not for the first time, why she had decided to stay with him all these years.

Chapter 12
1992

I woke up much earlier than normal since it was Katie's birthday. I laughed quietly to myself as I got up from my bed and turned off my wristwatch alarm. I had used it instead of my normal alarm to reduce the chances that someone else would hear it.

I debated what mayhem I should wreak upon the birthday girl to wake her up. It had to be something extra special though. I had never seen her, or anyone else, as excited as she had been lately. Considering that she was consistently happy and positive, and had been throughout her entire life, that was *really* saying something.

She had been counting down the days, to this day, for weeks. Crossing off days on the kitchen calendar. Chattering about it incessantly...birthday, birthday, birthday. I didn't understand her sudden need to be thirteen or what benefits it was going to yield. You couldn't drive or look for fun jobs until you were sixteen; you couldn't vote, claim to be an adult, or go to college until you were eighteen; and of course, you couldn't drink (legally) until you hit the ripe old age of twenty-one.

Thirteen wasn't even when Katie would start high school—she was only going to be in the eighth grade this coming year. Not that high school was all that great. I had looked forward to it for football and because there were older girls. I don't think that either of those things was of much interest to her.

I tiptoed down the hallway to Katie's room. As usual, she had left her door open a little bit and had a nightlight on in her room, so it was easy to make my way without turning on any lights. She didn't use the nightlight because she was scared—she was too mature for that—she left it on in case our parents felt like they should come check on her.

She had always amazed me.

So what is so special about being thirteen? I wondered. *Could she be interested in a guy?* I supposed it was a possibility. I knew that her and her friends might talk about a boy they thought was cute or whatever. But it seemed unlikely that it would drive the kind of jubilance we had been seeing.

There was also, just being able to say that you were a *teen*ager. And, really, that was just a bragging right; it wasn't even something with substance that you could sink your teeth into, and Katie had more substance than most adults I knew.

No, I decided, *there isn't any good reason to be excited about thirteen. There is just no good reason.*

That's when it hit me. *Katie is probably so happy because there is no reason to be happy!* That was just the type of crazy, positive thinking that might be true. Katie was excited about being thirteen in spite of what Earth and all of its other inhabitants thought.

To make matters worse, Mom had been secretly making arrangements for a surprise birthday party for weeks, maybe even months. There was the frenzy of excitement and energy from my sister daily, center stage; and then there was the frenzy of excitement and energy from my mother, daily, behind the curtains.

I loved my sister—I was happy for her—but I just didn't get it. In the end I concluded that it must also have something to do with hormones. A chick thing...had to be a chick thing.

I crept the last few inches to Katie's door and peeked in at her. She lay on her back in the center of her bed with her covers pulled up to her armpits. The corners of her mouth were turned up slightly. *She's even smiling in her sleep,* I mused.

The big question: what should I do this year to wake her up?

The previous year, birthday number twelve, wasn't very inspired. I simply woke up early, got my mom and dad, and we dog-piled her and tickled her awake.

The year before that, I got Scott to help me pick her

mattress up with her on it, and we moved it outside to the back yard. That was tough, but luckily Katie is the heaviest sleeper that ever lived. She woke up and birds were chirping just feet away.

The years before were all pretty similar, all of them juvenile, but still fun.

This year, I decided to try something I figured would be easy and fun. I went down to the kitchen and got the can of whipped cream that was in the refrigerator. I took one of my mother's large mixing bowls and emptied the can into it...I didn't want the can to make the *hisssss!* noise in Katie's room.

Then I grabbed the cheap 35mm camera that we used whenever we didn't want to carry our expensive and bulky Minolta SLR. *Now I know why thirteen is so special,* I thought and chuckled quietly. As I was about to go back to Katie's room with my supplies, I heard voices float down the hallway from my dad's where-I-hide-and-smoke room: his office.

That's strange, I thought, inching closer and listening. My dad was rarely awake this early—a luxury afforded to him by his inheritance—and I was very curious about what he was doing.

I walked quietly down the hallway and the voices grew louder as I drew near. I recognized my mother's voice, too. They were having an argument.

I moved as close as I dared. The door was slightly ajar and I didn't want to be busted eavesdropping.

"Lainey, I said I was sorry," my father said.

"I just can't take it anymore, William. I can't take it." The silence was sudden and I wondered what was happening...then I heard my mother sobbing. Finally, she spoke, "William...I want a divorce."

"What? Lainey, come on..."

"I want a divorce. This time I mean it."

My father made a strange sound and then he started begging: "Please, Lainey. Please. It's over. I'll change. I'll do whatever you tell me. Just please, don't go."

He was answered with silence.

"Please don't take my kids away from me," he pleaded.

"You're hardly there for them, William! Other fathers would love to have children that wonderful, and you don't even seem to care. And, they adore you, though for the life of me, I can't figure out what you have done to deserve it."

"I do care. Just give me another chance. Please."

Another silence: longer this time.

"Okay."

"Okay? Okay! Thank you, Lainey. You won't regret it. I'll be a good husband and a good father."

Their conversation sounded like it might be ending, so I hurried back the way I had come and up the stairs to Katie's room. I tiptoed in, with my hands still full of the tools for mischief, but I no longer felt much like playing any jokes on her. I felt sad.

I sat down next to her on the bed and thought about my parents and this situation. My mother had told him she wanted a divorce. It sounded as if it wasn't the first time it had come up. I knew my dad could be a jerk, but I was also floored by the tone in my mother's voice when she told him he didn't deserve his kids.

"Jack!" Katie exclaimed. Scaring me half to death.

"Ah!" I didn't have time to think, and I didn't want Katie to discover that I was anything but happy on her birthday, so I took the bowl of whipped cream in my hands and put it on Katie's head. Upside down.

"Jack!" She squealed, fluffy white goop dripping down all around her. Then she started laughing and she took some of the cream and smashed it on my face. I started laughing, too, and for the time being, I pushed away the conversation I had overheard.

"Happy birthday, Katie!"

Chapter 13
Friday, August 10th, 2012

Samantha and I simultaneously grabbed our respective door handles on the French doors leading outside to the backyard at my parents' house. We opened them wide, curtains billowing in the sudden wind, and stepped through. We left the doors wide open as we stepped out into the light of the afternoon...

We walked slowly across the patio. The weather was immaculate and birds were fluttering here and there. Despite the Disney quality setting, I could sense that something was wrong; some evil thing was waiting for us. I stopped and looked to my left and there was my father, in his favorite poolside lounger, sipping a drink. It was a beer...with one of those little umbrellas, that only belong in island drinks, poking out of the top. He gave us a wave and a smile and then went back to his drink. I was suddenly uneasy...uneasy...

I turned slowly and looked to my right, at Samantha, and my heart rate increased exponentially. Samantha's eyes were dull and there was a filmy, milky substance covering the iris of each eye. They sat like two cloudy brown pearls, devoid of life, staring out from deep within the shell of a clam.

I turned and looked ahead of me then, at the pool, and I took a few hesitant steps forward. I could see something beneath the water in the deep end of the pool. The edges were blurry, indistinct, and I couldn't identify what it was by the shape. But, some intuitive part of me knew that whatever it was, it was there because of me, waiting for me.

In slow motion I dove into the pool and pumped my arms, swimming with all my might, toward the shape huddled near the drain. A sense of déjà vu swallowed me. I could see clearly now that it was a small boy in the water, which heightened my growing sense of urgency. I tried to move quickly, but I couldn't; I didn't have control over my own limbs. It was like swimming in clear molasses.

Time was an enigma—there was no way of measuring it—but

it took much too long to traverse the short distance that separated me from the child.

Finally...I reached the boy and tried to put my arms around him to pull him up to safety; however, he didn't budge. My hands slipped around on his body while I tried to figure out what was preventing me from pulling him to the surface. I moved around to get a better grip and came face to face with the boy. That's when I realized it was Jacob.

Sadness threatened to overwhelm me while I looked into his perfect little face. Time stopped, an ominous threat to us both.

That's when Jacob's eyes snapped open...

"Jack! Wake up!"

"Oh, my God!" I opened my eyes. Samantha was standing next to me with an anxious look on her face. "What...?" I asked, confused, heart pounding.

"You were having a bad dream, Jack. It was just a bad dream. You were calling for Jacob..."

That's when it came back to me. We were in the hospital. Samantha and I had stayed overnight even though, technically, this was against policy. We were granted a lot of flexibility for three reasons: our doctor was compassionate to our situation; my mother volunteered in virtually all big hospital events through the year; and...my *father* had given some money recently to the hospital. They had even given us an extra hospital bed, which my wife had slept in. *It must have been a lot of money,* I assumed.

"Hmph," I groaned. *If it weren't for him, we wouldn't be here.*

Samantha and I moved about, brushing teeth, washing faces, and freshening up a bit. I noticed that although Jake had not awakened, he definitely looked a little healthier and it wasn't just my imagination. He had continued to make improvements through all of the little tests the doctors used to gauge that sort of thing.

And...it wasn't very long before the doctors arrived.

There were a round of *good mornings* and the shaking of

hands. The doctors told us that they would have Jacob undergo a series of tests and scans that would give a more in-depth view of his brain activity and function. They urged us to get out and get some fresh air; they would be gone with Jacob all morning.

Samantha and I aren't very good at listening. After the nurses wheeled Jacob away, we went about performing mindless activities while we waited for the test results. Aside from the occasional bathroom break, and a quick trip to the hospital cafeteria, we stayed where we were.

Jacob was gone for a few hours, but the doctors brought him back intact, with preliminary results in hand. There was also a new doctor in tow behind Dr. Nichols.

"Hello Mr. and Mrs. Leonard, this is Dr. Reid, one of the top neurologists in the state."

"Hello, Doctor," I said, shaking his hand. It was a good, firm grip—a sign of trustworthiness, according to my father.

"Hi." My wife also shook his hand.

"Good morning, it's nice to meet you both," he said. "I know you are anxious to hear the news, so I won't waste any time.

"All of the tests we have performed have had positive results. By that I mean that they all indicate that your son's brain is functioning normally and there are no indications that Jacob's brain is *not* functioning."

Samantha and I both sighed audibly with relief.

"We performed basic tests as well as some that aren't so basic. Upon arrival, of course, we checked his eyes with a bright light. A functioning brain will receive a message from the optic nerve that there is bright light and respond by sending a signal to the pupil to make it smaller in response. His response was perfect.

"We altered his ear temperature, performed a check on his gag reflex, and did other tests which all confirm neurological function."

"Great," I said.

"Yes, these are good signs," Dr. Reid continued. "We

have performed many of these tests more than once and this morning, as we discussed, we performed a PET scan to check the function of his brain. The results were, again, very positive.

"However, I do want to caution you that positive results on these tests only indicate that the brain is functioning. Unfortunately, when the brain is deprived of oxygen, well, there is always the chance of permanent impairment. It could be minor…or it could be more serious."

Sam and I nodded and I slid my arm around her waist.

"But, we won't know the specifics until Jacob gains consciousness."

"Do you know when that will be? Any estimate…" I asked.

"No. It could be a matter of days, but it could also be weeks, or longer. I don't want to give you false hope by predicting something unpredictable. Keep a good positive outlook and be hopeful. That's the best thing we can all do right now."

"Of course," Samantha said.

"And just because he is unconscious doesn't mean he cannot hear you! Make sure you talk to your son. Tell him you love him and can't wait to see him. Talk to him about his favorite television shows and video games. The studies are very lopsided in favor of this being good for the patient…and it's good for the parents, too!"

I nodded. "You bet, Doc." I was good at staying positive—it was one of the reasons I was into marketing and public affairs—and this gave me something to focus on. I secretly vowed to talk to Jacob all day long.

We talked to the doctors for another 10 or 15 minutes, and listening to their words and reflecting on the situation, I realized just how fortunate we were to have them on our side. They were professional and friendly. More than that: they were genuinely concerned about our son, and us, too.

As Dr. Nichols and Dr. Reid made their exit, my mom popped into the room. She had bright flowers in her hand, the product of her own green thumb and garden. "Hey, guys."

"Hi, Mom," we greeted her. "Did you get some sleep last night?" Samantha asked.

"I did, thank goodness, but did *you*?" she returned. "Jake's going to need strong parents when he wakes up."

"We did...*sort* of. You must have some serious pull here. Not only were we allowed to stay, but they also brought in an extra bed..."

"Oh, well, I guess they know us pretty well." She cleared her throat and looked at me, saying, "Your father has contributed a lot to this hospital in the past..."

I sighed.

"Jack..."

"Yes, Mom," I replied, a little exasperated. I knew she was going to bring up my father, possibly our confrontation, and I wasn't ready to address that...not yet.

"Now, Jack, I have a favor to ask you. Okay? I need you not to get upset."

"I'll try, Mom."

"Okay. Your father is out in the hallway and would like to see Jacob..."

I could feel myself reddening—a trait that only reared its head in special moments—and my defenses went up. I was rarely without words, but this was one of those moments.

"Now, Jack, let's just not do this. Not right here, and not right now. This isn't the right time or place to argue about blame." Her tone was stern—a tone I wished suddenly she had used with my father more through the years—and I knew I wasn't going to argue.

But, it didn't mean that I had to accept the situation with open arms either.

"Fine, Mom. I'll go to the house for a little while. I need to shower anyway."

She looked like she was about to say something...then decided against it. "Okay, Jack." She rushed over then and gave me a big hug: a momma hug. It caught me completely off guard and relieved the tension in the room. She hugged Katie and me all the time when we were kids, but she had a special hug that she saved for the *really tough* times in our lives; she called them momma hugs.

Of course, this wasn't the first time a situation involving my dad led to a momma hug; but, the last time was a few decades earlier.

"Thanks, Mom," I told her.

"You're welcome, Jacky. I'll call you when I leave with your dad."

"Okay. Thank you."

I kissed Samantha, told her that I would be back soon, and left the room.

I passed my dad in the hallway, just outside the door to Jacob's room. He looked hopeful and I thought about my mother. I acknowledged him with a nod, which he returned, and that was it. I could see, however, that the interplay between us, minor as it was, gave him some solace, and he walked a little easier the few remaining steps to Jacob's door. I continued down the hallway toward the exit.

It could have been worse; there was so much more I could have told him. But, surprisingly, I decided against it. My mother was levelheaded—a good person—with good instincts and a profound sense of right. I think that her invisible hand led me to make the right decision.

My father would never know that he owed that peaceful crossing of paths to his wife. He probably owed her for a thousand unknown moments like that.

Chapter 14
Saturday, August 11th, 2012

We woke up early. To be truthful, it's hard to say whether we slept at all. I know we laid down in the same spots as we had the night before; I took the chair and Samantha used the extra bed that the staff, again, promptly brought in at the end of visiting hours.

I know that our eyes were closed (sometimes) and there were a few hours when neon lighting didn't stare ominously from above. There was ample glow from Jacob's rack of monitoring devices to allow movement around the room (and prevent sleep).

I stood and stretched, but it was painful...my neck and my back were aching...an indicator that I had been in that uncomfortable damned chair long enough.

So, yes, I suppose we did what people refer to as *sleeping*, though time is relative when your son is in a coma. Everything takes too long and you never have enough time; however, it feels like you spend an incredible amount of time waiting. It's as if the hours of each day were redistributed, allocating fewer hours for sleep and more hours for unproductive inactivity and worry.

Samantha was up and moving. I joined her at the sink and we brushed our teeth in silence. She gave me a smile, but it was one of those sad ones.

When we finished cleaning ourselves up, Samantha took my hand, and we walked over to Jacob's bedside. He looked very peaceful this morning. I choked down, and shook off, the litany of bad things that popped into my mind:

This isn't fair.
I shouldn't have left him...
Why Jake?

I shook my head, forced those unsettling thoughts away,

and tried to harness positive feelings to replace them. I watched as Samantha leaned in and gave Jake the biggest hug that she could, considering the situation.

"Happy birthday, Jakey," she said. Her tone was normal, but she really enunciated the words, as if she were speaking to someone reading lips. I noticed that we had both been doing that. We hoped that our words would penetrate down into Jake's subconscious...and that he would really hear us.

"Happy birthday, buddy," I told him (extra enunciation), then I hugged him. When I pressed our torsos together I could feel his heart beating. It was a comforting sensation—his heart felt like it was healthy and strong. I stayed there against him for a bit, then let go reluctantly.

"He's an angel, Jack."

"He is," I agreed.

We went about our same routine that morning. Doctors and nurses moved around carrying charts and clipboards, performing maintenance on people, like auto mechanics for humans. Jake had some additional minor tests, as well, which yielded further prognoses of healing and improvement.

When a nurse came in and announced that she would bathe Jacob, Samantha and I decided to test out the coffee in the cafeteria. We weren't big coffee drinkers—Sam occasionally had a flavored coffee from Starbucks—but neither of us wanted to disturb the nurse while she did her job. I figured it was a tough enough thing to do without parents there to nitpick and henpeck.

The first thing that both of us noticed was the sunshine. It was pouring into the cafeteria through large windows. We gravitated over to them and stood there, basking in the heat and light. I observed that others in the room were standing near windows, too, enjoying that big ball in the sky that gave us all life.

"Finally...windows." Samantha loved natural light. Going hours without sunlight was something she had never done well...it made her a little cranky. She roved our house each morning opening shades and raising blinds.

"Mmm. Yeah."

We stood there and opened up like budding flowers turning into the sun's rays. It removed some of the shadows, both literal and figurative, that had been following us around.

"Coffee?" I asked her.

"*Mmm-hmm.*"

We wandered over to the coffee preparation area, filled our white Styrofoam cups from the silver restaurant-style machines, and rummaged through a veritable smorgasbord of little containers filled with powders and granules, all designed to make coffee taste like anything but coffee.

A couple of greenbacks into the hands of the cashier, and we made our way to one of the tables engulfed in that yellow flame. I saw that about half of the tables, diagonally across the room, were bathed in sunshine. The other tables were in shade. It amused me to see that only the tables on the bright side were occupied.

"Look at that," I motioned with my hand at the bright half of the room. "Half the room is lit up by the sunshine and that is the half where people are sitting."

"The absence of windows is probably getting to everyone. The employees are probably continuously on the verge of depression."

"And the stupid fluorescent lights..."

"Yeah. Awful."

We sat down at our table, each taking sips of our coffee. It was hot—*piping hot*—exactly how I liked it those rare moments I drank coffee. I took another sip, and I realized that it was delicious, too. I heard Samantha make an appreciative noise, almost sensual, and I raised my eyebrows.

"They must put something in it," I told her. "I've never had coffee that good...and this is *hospital* coffee, you know?"

"True. It's better than Starbucks. Did you use any creamer in yours?"

"Nah. You know me. Black."

"Just like your hangover days from college."

"You bet," I said, grimacing as I let some more of the scalding liquid pass down my throat. It was a good burn.

"I think it's so yummy because we're so beat up. I was feeling exceptionally dreadful until just a few minutes ago."

I nodded my head. "Let's get another cup." If coffee was what we needed right now to feel a little better, then I figured we might as well drink our fill. "It helps to be out of that awful lighting in there. Do you want to step outside for a few minutes? Just get some fresh air?"

"Sure. I love you, Jack," she paused and looked up at me. "You know...I love you for what you did for Jake...at the pool. That was amazing." She reached up and touched the side of my face and I pushed my cheek into her palm. Samantha's eyes were wet with tears, but hadn't released yet, so I took my thumbs, and with my hands in the shape of wings, wiped the tears away before they fell.

"Come on, lady...let's take a walk."

As we wandered around the grounds of the hospital, a small patch of green amidst the shopping malls and highways, I thought about Jacob. I hoped that he would have the chance, some day, to meet the girl of his dreams, just like I had. *He deserves the perfect son,* I thought, smiling to myself. A boy who is intelligent yet innocent, but not naïve. A boy adventurous and spirited; a kid who shows unabashed love to his parents when the others don't anymore because it *isn't cool.*

He deserved a son just like himself...what I had been blessed with.

Our walking loop came to a close and we passed through the electric doors into the lobby of the hospital. A mild sense of oppression settled on me as we entered the no-window zone and walked toward Jake's room. It felt just a little harder to breathe.

"I wonder if there has been any study on the long-term effects of daily exposure to this type of lighting," I said.

"I don't know," Samantha replied distractedly.

"Sorry...just rambling with no point." I pushed open Jake's door and we walked into his room.

"Hi, guys..." Katie ran over to hug us when we got inside. "I'm so sorry that I couldn't be here sooner."

"Oh, Katie..." Samantha said. This time there wasn't any stopping the tears.

"Sis..." I said, hugging her back tightly.

"Oh, you two! I've been thinking about you night and day. They didn't want me to take any time off from work, but I told them they could fire me—I'm leaving."

"Sis, you didn't have to do that..."

"No, Jack," she said very seriously, halting my objection. "I *did* have to do that. You two are the best parents, and you're both strong, but you need your family right now.

"I know you remember what Mom used to say...I've heard you say it to Jacob: nothing is more important than family. Nothing."

"You're right," I told her. "Thanks for being here, Sis."

"Hey, no problemo, big brother. Samantha...have you been holding up well?" She was holding both of Sam's hands when she asked. Sam nodded. Katie nodded empathetically and they shared a profound look of understanding between them. It might not seem possible, but somehow my family had a stacked deck when it came to good mothers. Katie, Samantha, and my mom were the best.

"Hello!" Elaine Leonard called out, pushing backwards into the room.

Her arms were overflowing, stacked absurdly high with cake and presents, and I ran over to help her.

"Oh, man, Sam...our presents..." I started when I realized that they were birthday presents for Jake she was carrying.

"Samantha told me where they were hidden...some of these are yours," my mom answered. "Let's set them on that table with wheels." Katie, Samantha, and I each grabbed something and went about setting things up around the room and Jacob's bed.

My mother removed the canvas bag that she had slung over her shoulder and began to pull out various decorations: crepe streamers, banners, and balloons. There was even a pack of those silly noisemakers that you blow and the little paper unrolls and shoots out.

"Can I help?" I asked her.

"Of course, dear." She sounded pleased. We all joined in and my mom assigned us little tasks. Just like that, I felt like a kid again with a chore from mommy.

For half an hour we were all busy cutting, inflating, taping, and hanging. When we were done, it didn't even look like a hospital room anymore. It looked like the kids' party room at the local bowling alley or something.

"Good job, y'all," my mother said looking around, pleased with our handiwork. She walked over to Jacob's bed, rubbed her hand through his hair, then leaned down and gave him a kiss on the forehead. "Happy birthday, Jake. Grandma loves you."

Katie joined Mom and smiled down at Jake. "Aunt Katie loves you, too, Jake. Happy birthday, big guy." She also went in for a kiss on the cheek.

Samantha and I were hanging back, watching, when the door opened again giving us another surprise: Scott Thompson.

"Bro..." Scott said, crossing the room quickly. I opened up my arms for the standard man-hug, but Scott went in for the real thing and hugged me tightly. It startled me. I couldn't be sure, but I think that it was a first in our nearly thirty years of friendship. I hugged him back.

"You should have called me." He sounded pretty choked up.

"Ah, man..." I was feeling it, too.

"Dude. I forgive you, but you know I'm right." A couple of tears fell freely from his face when we parted. His eyes were puffy and bloodshot, which made me suspect that he had already shed more than a few tears. Scott walked over to Samantha and hugged her too.

My mom: "Hi, Scotty."

"Mrs. L..." Another hug. More tears.

Katie: "Hello, Scott."

"Hi, Katie." More hugs and more tears. It was as if his hugs induced tears.

The power of Scott's entrance shouldn't have surprised me. He was my best friend.

But, it wasn't just that. This was more than best friends. My parents were like his parents. My son was like his son. He was protective of my little sister, Katie. And, my wife was our best friend, too. He never...and I mean never...treated us with anything except love.

"Glad you're here, man."

"I'm glad I'm here, too. Oh, yeah...before I forget..." He pulled a small present from his cargo pocket and handed it over to me. "For our dude."

We pulled up around Jacob, the whole lot of us, and wiled away an hour sharing stories about Jake. They were the tales of mischief, courage, innocence, and love that we had all shared a hundred times before, but we told them again. I think it helped all of us cleanse our souls a little bit.

Just when I thought the surprises were done, the door opened again, slowly...

It was my dad.

The talking tapered off and several throats were cleared in succession. You could almost hear the cliché scratch of the record player.

He looked at us and his eyes begged for acceptance. I was torn inside about what to do. I hated him for not taking care of Jacob at that critical time when he needed it. It was the single biggest failure in life that I could imagine. I wondered if everyone in the room knew the story. My mother had learned discretion—obviously—having been with my father for almost forty years. I guessed that Scott and Katie didn't know.

At the same time, he was my dad, and that meant something to me. I didn't want to love him...I wanted to hate him. But, I'm a father, too, and I couldn't imagine something driving a permanent wedge into my relationship with Jacob. That would crush me.

And Dad loved me, too. I knew that.

No, he wasn't the best person, but he was family. And...nothing is more important than family.

I looked over at my mom. She was watching me. I think she could see the decision in my eyes and she nodded her head approvingly.

With a mighty effort I got up and walked over and stood facing my dad. We stood that way looking at each other for a moment. I could see the pain in his eyes; maybe, he could see the pain in my eyes, too.

I noticed that everyone kept their distance, cautious, like they were about to witness two bears fight and didn't want to get between us.

"Jack..." his voice cracked, he opened his arms, and I let him hug me for a few seconds. "I'm sorry," he whispered in my ear.

I returned his hug then. It wasn't perfect—life isn't perfect—but family is family. There was unfinished business between us, but it could wait.

The others stood up, came forward, and surrounded us. There were more hugs and a few fresh tears. I looked around at all the most important people in my life: Samantha, Jacob, Katie, Scott, and my parents.

"Hey," I said. "It looks like Team Leonard is back together."

"And, *Scott*..." Scott chimed in.

"Scotty, brother, you *are* part of Team Leonard," I told Scott. I looked over at my dad, "right, Dad?"

"That's right, Scotty...that's right."

My mother came and gave me a hug. Her eyes told me *thank you*; mine told her *you're welcome*.

We sat back down in a semi-circle around Jake's bed and my family gradually recommenced with the storytelling. I'm pretty sure that everyone thought it was good for Jacob. I sure did. It was painful, but a lot of good things are painful, I suppose. Childbirth, for example, is possibly the greatest pain a person can feel, yet it results in new life.

I was mentally and emotionally drained. It had been surprise after surprise today: Katie's arrival; Scott's arrival; Mom's decorating zeal; and finally my dad's appearance. Combined with the already tenuous situation we were in, it was almost too much.

"Not sure I can handle any more surprises today," I mentioned to Sam.

"Me either," she agreed and yawned.

Except, there's always room for another surprise, isn't there? You bet there is.

~~~~~

"Let's sing *Happy Birthday* to Jake. What do you think?"

"That sounds fine, Mom," I told her. "Sam?"

"Yes. That would be nice."

"Okay. I'll get the cake and light the candles." My mom went and got everything ready and brought it back to Jake's bed. She put the cake down on the wheeled table that patients use to eat dinner and got out one of those really long, *Extended Reach* lighters. She always had a few of them around the house.

"Why do you always use those, Mom?"

"Oh, they're wonderful, Son. You know I like candles and it's just too hard to light them with a normal lighter. Plus your dad likes them for his grill."

"What?" I asked confused. "Why would Dad need a lighter for his grill?"

"He didn't tell you? He's using gas now."

I looked at my dad, shocked again. "Really?"

"Yeah, it's just easier, Son. I keep a charcoal grill, too, but you know, only for guests."

I sat back in my chair while Mom lit the candles.

"Everybody ready?" she asked. We all replied in one way or another that we were. "Okay, then...happy birthday, to you...happy birthday to you...happy birthday, dear Jakeyyyy...happy birthday to you."

"I'll blow out the candles and make a wish for Jake," I told everyone. I walked over to the table and stopped just in front of the cake.

I closed my eyes tight and made my wish for Jacob. When I opened my eyes, I blew out all of the candles. On any other birthday, everybody would cheer and clap, however, for this one...we were mostly quiet. I noticed that a few sets of eyes were closed. I looked up and studied the smoke from the eleven candles, as it drifted toward the ceiling...

"Dad..." Jacob croaked.

"Oh, my God!" Samantha squealed. "My baby!"

There was a flurry of movement and voices as everyone leapt out of their seat, babbling excitedly all at once.

Mom and Katie simultaneously: "Jakey!"

Scott: "Hey, buddy!"

Dad: "Oh, Jake!"

I leaned my head in and put it against Jake's head and I cried. "Hey, buddy," I whispered. Samantha was on the other side of him soon, pressing her head into his, too.

"I love you, Jacob," she said. "Oh, I love you so much!"

"Me, too, dude, I love you, too."

I heard Katie behind us announcing that she was going to get the doctors.

Jake smiled at us, dreamily, like he was just waking up from a deep sleep instead of from a coma. "Dad?"

"Yeah, buddy?"

"What'd you wish for?"

The happy kind of tears popped into my eyes then. "It just came true, buddy. My wish just came true."

Chapter 15
1991

Scott and I were sitting quietly in my dad's truck. Classic rock was playing softly through the radio, but I wasn't really listening, and I doubt that Scott or my dad were listening either.

My father hadn't really said a word to either of us. I couldn't tell whether he was angry or just giving us space. But, I had seriously let him down. I had let everyone down that night.

We had just played *the* biggest game of our young lives: the state finals. It was supposed to be the culmination of everything we had practiced, played, and worked so hard for, but it didn't work out that way.

I wasn't sure that I would ever forget the surprise and hurt on everyone's faces when the final whistle blew. We had come close and been beaten—not by a better team—but because of the mistakes I made. I cost the team...*the whole city*...the state championship.

I stared out of the passenger window at all of the lights you find on a Texas highway at night: streetlights, strip malls, taillights, and the glowing consoles inside other vehicles.

How did I let myself mess up that bad? I wondered. I shook my head. It just didn't make any sense. I had been so arrogant. I changed the coaches' plays on the fly and went with what I thought was best.

They were bad decisions.

I had an interception and fumbled twice, as well. In every way I had choked—big time. I had let things go to my head more and more through the season. All the wins, the articles in the paper, and all of the newsreel highlights—I let it get to me.

Our head coach gave the team the standard you-lost-but-you're-still-winners talk at the end of the game. Most of the players weren't making eye contact with me. It wasn't something that I was accustomed to…it was a horrible feeling.

Then the coach released everyone to shower up. Except for me. He made it very clear to me how disappointed he was in a private lecture.

"Jack, you put yourself before the team. Day one, Son. I told you on day one that you never put yourself before the team. I don't mind mistakes on the field, but I won't have a bunch of individuals out there who play for themselves and not the team. When you do, you are disloyal to all of us," he said and paused. He leaned closer to me and lowered his voice: "You betrayed your team, Jack."

I didn't say a word. Not a single word.

"It's your junior year. You played well the last three years. I don't plan on kicking you off the team. But you need to think very seriously about what happened tonight and what has been happening to you the past couple of months if you want to play your senior year. You hearin' me, Jack?"

"Yes, Coach."

He eyeballed me for a solid ten seconds, at least…maybe more. Then he shook his head and released me. "Go shower up, Jack. We'll talk more later."

It was the quietest locker room I had ever been in. Some of the guys gave me a nod—the ones that forgave easily—but most just went about their business and got out of there.

I sat in my dad's truck and stared at the different lights, cars, and buildings. I had let it all spiral out of control and the lights of a Texas highway don't have many answers for that. I caught Scott's eye in the side mirror and he shrugged and tilted his head to one side.

"Jack?" my dad said.

"Yes, Sir?"

"Awful quiet in here." He was sober tonight: a rarity. And exceptionally lucid. He was so excited about the state finals that he hadn't had a drink at all that day. It was a small miracle…one which fueled my guilt.

"Dad…I *am* sorry about how things…went tonight."

"You don't need to apologize to me, Jack."

"But, I let you down…"

"No. You didn't let *me* down, I'm just your dad. But, you did let your team down…and you let yourself down, too. Those are hard words to hear…I *know* it. But sometimes you have to hear hard things." He stopped talking, turned the radio off, and turned his head to the side as he said, "Scott?"

"Sir."

"It'll do you good to hear this, too. Here's Billy Leonard's philosophy on this one. It's nothin' original…other people say these things, but this is how I organize it all in *my* head."

"Yes, Sir."

"Son, everyone makes mistakes. Little mistakes. Big mistakes. Mistakes all the same." He looked over at me, "When you make mistakes, there are a few things you need to do to make things right.

"One, be a man, and own up to your mistake. That doesn't mean you have to apologize, necessarily. It means you let people know where you stand. You were wrong. You tell them you were wrong.

"Two…you have to actually believe the first part. If you're just giving lip service to people, they're gonna know it, or they're gonna figure it out. If you don't accept that fact, you're already lost.

"Three, you need to fix it. Make it right. There's no one-size-fits-all answer for how to do that. Making things right is different in every situation. Sometimes you have to prove yourself all over again. Sometimes it *is* an apology. Sometimes it's the combination of a lot of things. You figure that out when the time comes.

"If you do those things, Son, and people don't forgive you, well…you've done what you can. Move on and don't make that mistake again. Life's just too short to waste time in situations like this."

I thought about what he said for the rest of the drive home. He was right. When you make mistakes that affect other people you had to admit you made a mistake, fix it, and move on.

Chapter 16
Sunday, August 12th, 2012

Samantha and I shared another night in the hospital. We hardly slept at all, but this time that was fine. We stayed up all night, whispering, like young girls at a sleepover. In the morning, I didn't mind the little aches here and there in my body. They didn't matter at all.

Because Jake was awake.

The night before, when Jake awakened from the coma, he had stayed awake nearly two hours. There was a sleepy, slow quality to his voice, and he lost focus now and then, but for the most part, he was our regular Jacob.

The doctors naturally came in multiple times to check on him. They said the key for now was allowing him time to rest and recover. We were warned about all of the things that could still go wrong or be *found* to be wrong with Jake. They told us that they would perform more tests in the following days and begin rehabilitation in whatever areas was needed, depending on the nature and extent of any damage found.

It was scary to hear them talk like that, but at the same time, it felt like anything would be a walk in the park compared to what we had been through...as long as Jacob was alive.

"I love you, Jack." Samantha was absolutely radiant; her smile could kill.

"I love you, too," I replied. "God, you're beautiful in the morning...even when you haven't showered for two days."

Samantha laughed quietly: "Thank you...I *think*."

"You're welcome. There's plenty more where that came from, too."

"I can't wait."

"I know."

We sat down next to Jacob after we cleaned up, anxious to be there when he woke up again. We didn't have long to wait…within an hour I had the pleasure of watching his eyelids flutter open. "How you doing, buddy?"

"Hey, Dad…hey, Mom."

"Hi, honey!" Samantha gave him a good hug. He lifted up his injured hand to return it and said, "Oh, ow!"

"Careful, buddy. Your hand is a little messed up there. You'll have to take it really easy for a while. Okay?"

"Yeah. Sure, Dad." He licked his lips, which were a little chapped even though we had put some lip balm on them. "Can I have some water?"

A chill ran through my body at the thought of Jacob wanting to drink water. Life is full of small ironies. "Yeah, let me get you some. Take it easy though…just sip it." I poured him a glass and held it up to his mouth. He put out his functional hand, and we both held on to the glass as he sipped water.

"Thanks, Dad." He licked his lips and said, "That's, like, the best water I ever had." Then he smiled.

"Not bad for a hospital."

Part of our daily routine stayed the same that day: the doctors took Jacob for tests and returned with favorable results; we watched Jacob sleep several times; and Samantha and I shared cups of coffee in the cafeteria.

The rest of the day was different and exciting: Jake was back!

Katie, Scott, and my parents were with us much of the day and for the first time in several days nobody cried. My dad and I didn't speak much, but I accepted his presence without complaint or malice. We weren't healed, but the immediate tension was gone…undoubtedly assisted by Jacob's rapid recovery.

I didn't say anything, but I noticed that he was sober. Again.

That makes three visits to the hospital where he hasn't had anything to drink, I thought. *At least that I can tell.*

~~~~~

We were all huddled around again in the evening, just like the day before, except there were happy smiles on every face this time. No sad ones.

Well, except for Jake's smile...his looked a little confused.

"You okay, buddy?"

"Yeah, Dad, but I was wondering...what happened?"

The question caught me by surprise. "You mean, the reason you're in the hospital, buddy?" I asked him. "Do you not, um, remember what happened?"

"Hmm." Jake looked thoughtful. He furrowed his brows and thought about it for a moment. "No, Dad, I don't remember. Not everything. I remember you and Mom were going to Galveston...oh, yeah, and me and Grandpa were playing video games."

"Nothing else?"

"Mmm. No...not really. Sort of, like a dream I can't remember when I wake up. Sort of like that."

"Well...there was an accident. You were in Grandpa's pool and there was an accident and you were stuck under the water for a little bit. You got your fingers caught in the drain...I guess you were messing around down there..."

"No way! Really?" He looked thoughtful. "So, did I get myself out?"

"No, honey...you're daddy jumped in and pulled you out." Samantha was holding his hand.

"But, I was okay then, right, like I was breathing?"

Samantha and I looked at each other, but I wasn't sure how to answer. My mother cleared her throat and added: "Jakey...you're dad jumped in and pulled you out. And you weren't breathing.

"So, he did CPR on you...and he made you breathe

again."

"Wow," Jake said. He was genuinely...impressed. "Far out, Dad!"

Scott chuckled behind me and said, "Hell...err, I mean, heck yeah, dude. Far out. Your dad saved your life. This is going to be the coolest story to tell your buddies at school. The girls are going to love it, too."

"Scott..." Katie started, but she covered her mouth because she was smiling.

I was looking at the floor, embarrassed by the attention, when I felt a small hand on my forearm. I looked up and Jake was looking very intensely at me. It suddenly seemed that his 11-year-old eyes were much older. Like maybe he was the adult; and I was the child.

"Thanks, Dad."

I cleared my throat, "Of course, Jake...I love you."

"I love you, too."

There was a chorus of *I-love-yous* all around then. Everybody loved everybody. I loved that everybody loved everybody.

"You know, Jake, we've forgotten something very important."

"What's that, Grandma?"

"Why...your presents, Jakey!" She stood from her chair, smiling, and walked back to the table in the corner where all the presents were waiting, patiently, for Jake.

Chapter 17
Monday, August 20th, 2012

Jacob was discharged the following week...twelve days after he drowned.

Samantha and I had been at the hospital almost continuously during that time. Neither she nor I had wanted to leave Jacob alone. Minor discomforts (and questionable hygiene) were small sacrifices.

Hospital policy required that we bring Jacob to the car in a wheelchair. He seemed to think that was funny...an 11-year-old boy riding in a wheelchair when he felt fine...but he didn't complain. On the contrary, he embraced it as another life experience he might never have again.

He was wise beyond his years that way.

Jake wasn't surprised by the news that he wasn't allowed to swim for a while. He had, after all, damaged his hand and it needed time to heal. What went unspoken, was that his parents were also damaged and needed time to heal.

We had spared him the details of his drowning. He knew it happened, but he didn't know that his grandpa was asleep in a lounge chair. He knew Dad saved him, but he didn't know (or ask) what brought Dad back home in time to do that. He didn't ask the questions and we were happy not to answer. Samantha and I had discussed it and decided it would be best for the family to omit my dad's state of being and just roll with our arrival in the nick of time.

Back at my parents' house, there was a welcome home party waiting for Jake.

Katie had taken another day off from work (*they can fire me!*) and was there with her kids. Miranda and Mike Jr. were wearing party hats and called out *Happy Birthday* when we came into the house. A cheery vibe radiated from them.

Jake's best friend, Ryan, was there, too. They gave each

other some sort of secret handshake with different grips, and slaps, and fives. They used the word *dude* in just about every sentence. Then they *oohed* and *awed* over the cast they had put on Jake's hand to keep his fingers aligned. Ryan's mom, Paula, was in the kitchen watching, smiling, and having her standard glass of wine...she brought it as a gift...but I wasn't sure anyone else would get a glass.

Scott was there of course, so like Jake, my best friend was there too. The kids generally thought Scott was super cool. *How had he managed to have that affect on people his entire life?* I wondered. *He definitely won the genetic lottery in regards to being cool.* The kids all, at various points, climbed on him and called him *Uncle Scott*, a familial term of endearment they coined without any help from the adults.

My parents were there. My mother had whispered to me in conversation the day before, that Billy hadn't had a drink since *that day*. She was undoubtedly employing mom magic to curry favor with me on his behalf. She was ever the healer—the interminable seeker of balance—and I could only wonder what state our family would have been in without her strength these many years.

And there was my dad. His interactions were cautious but happy. It was bizarre seeing him that way since he was normally so outgoing. But *normal* had disappeared for him twelve days before. *Normal* had disappeared for all of us— momentarily—but it was coming back.

Billy Leonard, however, had the weight of our near-tragedy on his shoulders. It had happened under his watch. A watch he kept poorly because of his alcoholism...and because his behavior had been long accepted by all of us.

I watched him, watched his uncertainty, and I felt bad for him. Had I blamed him at first for what had happened? Absolutely. I was angrier than I had ever been when this first happened—my son was almost stripped from my life and this world forever—but the anger had subsided.

It could have happened to anyone, I thought to myself.

Jacob is a strong swimmer and we had all grown complacent when it came to supervising him in any swimming situation. How many times had we lost sight of him for three to six minutes at the beach? How many times had we gone in and out of the house while he was in our own pool, leaving him on his own for three to six minutes? How many times had Samantha and I been doing a hundred other small chores with our backs turned on him for the three to six minutes that they think he was under the water?

There was no good answer for it. *We're all guilty*, I thought.

"Hey, Dad...where are the rest of my presents?" Jake asked. His question gave me a welcome break from my own thoughts for a moment.

"Oh, hey buddy...I forgot...they're in the Rover. Give me a minute, I'll go grab 'em."

"Thanks, Dad," he said quickly and turned his attention back to Ryan, "Wait 'til you see what I got, it's *so* awesome."

"I'll help," Samantha said. We got up together and strolled through the front door to our vehicle. "It's great that everyone could be here."

"Yeah. We really have some great friends, Sam."

"We do."

We grabbed the gifts that Jake had opened the week prior at the hospital. It was a birthday I would never forget...helping my son tear the paper off many of the packages because he was tired. Comas can do a lot of weird things to people, as it turns out, and sapping their strength is one of them, even after a short period.

"Okay, dude, here they are...show Ryan what the birthday fairy got you this year!" I set the bags down on the coffee table in the living room.

"Dad! C'mon, you know there isn't any such thing as a birthday fairy."

"C'mon, you know the birthday fairy is real. You saw him that one year."

Jake laughed. "Dad, that was you."

Everyone crowded around and watched as Jake, literally singlehandedly, pulled his gifts out of bags to show Ryan. *Cool* and *awesome* were not words used sparingly.

Jacob had saved the best for last.

"It's the final count-down..." he sang and pulled open the final bag. "An iPad *and* an iPod!"

"That's so awesome!" Ryan exclaimed.

"Oh, boy..." Paula said under her breath, "I guess I know what we'll have to buy Ryan now on *his* birthday. You got him the iPod and the iPad?"

"Sorry. You never know with that birthday fairy...always causing trouble."

"Yes, that birthday fairy..." she lifted her eyebrows and took another sip (swallow) of wine.

"Well, Uncle Scott had something to do with that, too. He got him the iPod Touch...we got him the iPad. He lucked out twice." I looked sideways at Scott.

"That dude is on the move...needs something portable...they complement each other," Scott added.

Mike Jr., Miranda, Jake, and Ryan huddled together on the floor and began taking turns playing with Jake's new gadgets.

"Dad, can I download Angry Birds?"

"Sure, buddy."

"Um, it costs a dollar..."

"Ahhh...okay, well bring it to me and I'll enter my Apple ID."

"Ha ha ha," Scott laughed. "Jack, a few years back you mocked the Apple *fan boys* out there for their craze over Apple products. Now listen to you. *'Bring it to me so I can enter my Apple ID.'* You're the *fan boy* now."

I laughed at him as I entered my password into Jake's iPad and he ran back to the other kids. "Don't be a hater, bro. I guess I'm one of them now. I'm a fan boy."

"Yeah, you are."

"Life changes and sometimes you change with it," I replied. The adults continued talking and watching the kids. My dad didn't speak too much, but he smiled at whatever Jake did, and was always quick to give the kids an answer if they asked him something. I found myself drifting off in my thoughts again while I watched him, back to what I was thinking about earlier.

I was willing to concede that it could happen to anyone, but I also felt that my dad was a little guiltier in this situation due to being drunk. Jacob was in his care, and he drank so much that he passed out without a care in the world, while his grandson was *playing* in the pool...then *drowning* in the pool.

So, there it was. I didn't think it was a cut-and-dry accident, but how much responsibility was my dad's? I didn't know. *Clear as mud*, Grandpa Seth used to say.

The question that really burned inside me now, was whether I could forgive my dad and move on.

Chapter 18
Wednesday, August 22nd, 2012

"Hey, Dad. Can we talk?"

I was standing in the kitchen washing my dishes after having picked at a bowl of my mom's cereal for breakfast. I was nervous, but I probably wasn't going to have a better opportunity if I wanted to have this talk soon and in person. We had the house to ourselves.

While it was doubtful that anyone could actually *fire* Katie, she had returned to her job, since the worst was over. She had left amidst hugs and tears the night before. She gave Jake an exceptionally long hug from his Aunt Katie.

Samantha, my mom, and Jake were all at the hospital for a check-up and to work on transferring all of Jacob's documentation to our hospital in Austin. It looked as if Jacob's recovery was so favorable, *remarkably favorable* as the doctors put it, that we would be able to leave the coming weekend.

"Of course, Jack...of course..." My dad answered. He put aside his newspaper. I could see the weary, anxious look in his eyes and face. He knew what was coming. We had kept a peaceful distance between us since Jacob's recovery, but we both knew that wouldn't work forever. It wasn't healthy and it didn't provide closure.

I walked around the kitchen counter and over to the table. I looked at my dad for a second and thought about sitting down, but I didn't think I could do this sitting. I needed to keep moving, as an outlet for my own nervous energy.

"It's about Jacob...It's about everything that happened."

Billy Leonard looked like he was being shoved in front of a firing squad. His lip quivered and one of his eyes twitched every few seconds. I wasn't enjoying it. Being a man means doing a lot of things you don't enjoy.

"What happened to Jake...that hurt me more than

anything, Dad. Jake is so pure, so honest, so good…he's the greatest thing in my life.

"I've had a lot of time to think about it the past two weeks. What happened was an accident. I'm not saying that it wasn't. But it was an accident that happened while you were supposed to be looking out for him. He's just a kid. More than that, you were drinking. You were passed out, drunk, while that happened to my son. That just isn't right, Dad. You know? I mean, have you thought about that?

"I know you love Jake. I know you do. But there is this place in real life where people and ideas meet. They come together and sometimes they overlap and sometimes they just connect to each other. Those two areas, your love for your grandson, and your excessive drinking, aren't compatible. They've overlapped before and we were lucky that nothing happened. Hell, Dad, they've overlapped for me, and for Katie, and for Mom, our whole lives, and we've always just been lucky."

I had been pacing a little bit without taking my eyes from him. His head was down and I saw the tears on his cheeks. There had been so many tears lately. It was hard to see more. All those tears were like the waters that change the shape of rocks over the course of thousands of years. It seemed like they were changing the shape of us, of our lives, falling so frequently as they had.

"You lost my trust, Dad. You lost Samantha's, too. And I'm just not sure what the right thing to do is anymore. You really hurt my heart this time.

"But, I think that things can be okay, maybe, but it all depends on you.

"Somebody I love once told me that when you made a mistake, there were three things you had to do: admit your mistake; believe it; and make things right. Do you know who told me that, Dad?"

My dad slowly got up from his chair and looked me in the eyes. His eyes were still wet from crying, but something

185

had changed. A little of the life had come back into them. He nodded his head and kept his eyes locked on mine.

"I remember, Son. Jack…" He let out a long breath as if he had been holding it in and walked around the table until he was an arm's length away. "Jack, I messed up. It's the worst mistake I ever made, and…I've made a lot.

"I know that Jake could have died. Because of me. Because I wasn't there for him when he needed it. Just like that I almost lost him and I almost lost you. I'm sorry for that, Jack. I've never been sorrier."

He reached a hand out and set it on my shoulder and continued. "I wasn't a good father or a good husband. I know that, too. I was gone, a lot, when I should have been with you guys. I don't have any good excuse.

"I've screwed up nearly everything in my life that was important. I've been given second chances, and third chances, and so many damned chances that it's impossible to count…more than any man deserves. I've been the luckiest man in this world and I pissed it away like the beer that I drank for all those years…just pissed it away.

"But, Jack…Jack, I'm begging you…if you can find it in your heart to give your dad just one more chance. Just one more chance…I am going to spend the rest of my life making good on it."

He was standing right there in front of me and I wanted desperately to believe him. "Dad, I don't think I can handle anything like that again."

"I know. You won't have to. Just trust me once more, Jack."

I thought about it. I loved my dad and I believed in family. I regularly asked Jake: *what's the most important thing, buddy? Family*, he would answer and he was excited about that answer. Jake believed in that answer. I believed in that answer.

What example would I be to Jacob if I didn't give our family another chance…the opportunity to be survivors, stronger, always together?

I nodded my head: "Okay, Dad."

He hugged me, patted my back, and stepped back with wet eyes. A smile turned his mouth up at the ends and he said, "Jack, that's just music to these ears. You've always been a good man: the best. So much better than me. Thank you."

We sat down after that and talked quietly about all the little topics that hadn't been covered during the previous two weeks. All those things we had missed with each other. He hinted at his not drinking—wanted me to know he was trying—not knowing, of course, that Mom had already told me.

When Samantha, Jake, and my mom got back home an hour later, we were still sitting there talking. My mother studied me from the kitchen then smiled broadly. She had undoubtedly read the situation and knew that new beginnings were underway. Jake told us all about his hospital visit, where the doctors treated him like a miracle. He hugged my dad at one point and I saw pure pleasure in my dad's eyes.

There are no absolutes in this world. Things could change for the worse or for the better. But, for now, it seemed to me that we were off to a good start.

Epilogue: 2012

Texas has more than its share of old farm roads. Some of them are used routinely; and some of them are not. Some of those roads just connect one piece of farmland to another, providing a path for farmers on their John Deere tractors to get to their fields. Now and then, you'll see two or three generations of farmers in those tractors as fathers and grandfathers introduce their sons and grandsons to their livelihood, to their lifeline.

Billy knew those Texas roads, even the roads he had never seen or used himself. He knew them the way a veterinarian knows dogs without having seen a particular dog before. It's something in the blood, and in the spirit, that combines with experiences to create wisdom.

Billy was using one of those roads. He reached over for the cold can nestled in the cup holder and brought it to his lips.

"Hmm. I think I'm finally getting used to this," he said.

"What's that?"

"The Mt. Dew." He smacked his lips together a few times in an exaggerated way towards his wife. "Lainey...I sure love you," he told her.

"I love you, too, William."

"I know you do. There's no way that you could have put up with me all these years otherwise."

"Oh, Billy..."

"I'm serious, Elaine. I owe everything to you. I'm going to try and make it up to you every day for all those less-than-perfect years." He looked sideways across the cab of the truck at her and she smiled at him. It made him feel like a teenager again, the way she smiled. There was always this...*glow* that she had. It was the reason he first asked her out.

Yep, Billy felt like he had a new lease on life. He had thrown himself, almost manically, into being a good husband the past few months. His good behavior was being rewarded and it felt like they were on an extended honeymoon.

He returned the smile. "Let's go see Jake."

~~~~~

I saw my parents come into the gym and motioned them over to where we were seated. I got up to meet them and hugged them both.

"We're not too late, are we?" my dad asked.

"Nah.   They're   just   doing   some   preliminary announcements and warm-ups. Jake's over there," I said and pointed. My dad looked where I pointed and waved. Jacob was watching and waved back. He also gave us a thumbs-up, which made me laugh.   We always joked about *bringing back* the thumbs-up.

"Oh, there's my Jakey!" Mom waved excitedly and Jake waved back again.

The swim season had just started a few weeks before—and this match was against a small school—so the bleachers *should* have been half-full. Instead it was standing room only and the bleachers were *packed!* Well, except for the Leonards.

We had a section of front-row bleachers reserved for all of us.

One of the local newspapers had run a human interest piece on Jacob two weeks before, at the suggestion of some of the faculty. Jake and I had become instant celebrities in the community. He was the miracle kid and I was the hero. I'd be lying if I said it wasn't fun...it was...but it would have been nice to be able to turn off the popularity now and then.

I was nervous. It was Jake's first swim meet and he had only had a couple of weeks of conditioning prior to today. He had one finger that was crooked, one misshapen knuckle, and some little scars, but otherwise his hand was fully functional again.

Psychologically, there appeared to be no residual fear or trauma from his accident. He still had no memory of it. And, while this was probably what Samantha and I worried about most—Jacob having some sort of mental aftershock—the *head doctors* told us that we shouldn't hold Jake back if he was ready to swim again.

And, man, was he ready!

So, yeah, we were nervous.

But, the school was eager to have him on the team, not only because of his previous record as a strong up-and-comer in the swimmer's world, but also because of the public appeal of our story. We were the comeback family, the miracle family, and we definitely put some zest back into Texas swimming.

"I think Jake might be on the evening news," Samantha whispered to me. There was a 3-person news team from KVUE setting up in the corner. I doubted that was standard swim-meet fare.

"I think you're right. I just hope Jake is okay."

"Me too."

Just then I heard a familiar howl and looked over to the entrance. Scott was hooting loudly across the pool at Jake. Jake responded enthusiastically with a double thumbs-up as Scott strolled up to our spot on the bleachers.

"Bro!" he said.

"My brother from another mother," I replied, standing up to give him a man-hug.

"Hey, Sam."

"Hi, Scott." Another hug.

"Katie...little sis! Mom and Dad!"

"Hi, Scott...it's so great you could make it!" Katie told him.

My parents: "Hello, Scott."

"I wouldn't miss this for anything," he told us all, smiling broadly.

We chatted amongst ourselves with barely contained excitement, waiting for the match to kick off. Katie, Samantha, and I had all received raises at work—no joke—which seemed like too much of a coincidence to not be related to Jacob's accident.

My parents' marriage was moving with a passion and commitment from my father that was enviable. He was also a doting and attentive father and grandfather. Billy Leonard was a new man—another miracle we attributed to Jacob's accident.

And, Scott? Even Scott had some good luck he associated with Jake's accident...he met someone special on his flight out from Houston back in August. She was a flight attendant, so he was now visiting us regularly and enjoying a healthy relationship again. His ex-wife had mistreated him and it was a true pleasure to see him so serene: no one deserved it more.

The match finally kicked off, and we all turned our attention to the pool as the kids lined up along one end. They competed in different strokes. Normally, Jacob would have competed in several, but since he was just coming back, without much practice, he had decided to stick to just one event today: the individual medley.

The coach seemed a little doubtful—the individual medley was tough—but it was hard to argue with (deny) Jacob, the local miracle. He had defied all the odds already...he had *lived*.

So the coach was giving him a shot. He knew that he had time to change things up and have a good season, if he needed to make changes later, but the fans wanted Jacob for now.

When it was finally Jake's race, the whole family grew quiet. I had butterflies in my stomach—just like when I would start in football—and I closed my eyes and sent one quick, silent prayer upwards for Jake's safety. When I opened my eyes, Samantha was looking at me smiling.

"Did you just pray for your buddy?" she asked.

"Absolutely."

"Good. I did, too."

We both turned back to the pool and waited. The race started and Jake stepped forward two steps and hit what they called a *trophy* position then launched himself into the pool.

"Oh, man, did you see his entry?" I said aloud to no one in particular.

"Go, Jake!" Samantha shouted.

I heard my dad tell someone near him, "That's my grandson!"

There were multiple kids competing in the round, but it became apparent that three of them were battling for the win: Jake was one of them! I became so wound up that I couldn't move, I could only sit tensed up, my hands clinched tightly, much like my visits to the dentist. I watched my son move up and down the pool.

Jake was neck-and-neck with another kid as they moved out of the backstroke and into the final stroke: the freestyle. Jake was about an arm's length behind. It was then that I realized, that people all around me were screaming for Jake.

Even though Jake was behind, he had a powerful freestyle stroke, and they were soon even, moving to the end. Samantha was screaming beside me.

I focused on them as they came to the finish...

JAKE WON!

I stood up and bellowed "Jake!" a couple of times. KVUE was definitely going to have an exciting finish to show on the news tonight!

We could barely contain ourselves when they announced *"Jacob Leonard"* as the race winner over the loudspeakers. We rushed out of the stands and crowded around Jake, whose smile was larger than life.

"Team Leonard!" I said, picking Jake up and putting him on my shoulder, above the group that started to build up around us.

"And, Scott..." Scott replied on cue.

"Scotty," my dad said. "You are part of Team Leonard!"

We all embraced that little, wet son of mine, of ours, and laughed. We were just one small family in this world, and we weren't perfect. We knew bad times and we knew good times. We had gone to the brink of the cliff and looked over the edge. And...we made it. We made it.

ABOUT THE AUTHOR

Bart Hopkins is originally from Galveston, Texas, but has lived in Mississippi, Louisiana, Tennessee, South Korea, and Germany. He has also been on brief forays into Bosnia and Kuwait. He was born in the middle of the 1970s.

The author has a BS in Liberal Arts and an MA in Adult Education; he has served in the United States Air Force for nearly 19 years as a Meteorologist. For now, Bart writes when he can, in those spare moments between work, Scouts, and soccer games. One day soon, he hopes to devote all of his time to bringing the characters in his head to life.

Bart's passions include reading, traveling, photography, writing, and sharing time with his beautiful wife and three awesome children.

Texas Jack is Bart's second novel. His first, *Fluke*, was co-authored with a friend during their back-to-back deployments.
You can learn more about the author, and contact him, through his website: www.barthopkins.com. He's always happy to hear from readers.

Made in the USA
Charleston, SC
07 August 2013